# Search the Woods

a novel by
## Ben Zajdel

Stone Crow Publishing. Dallas, Texas.

*For Julie, who believes in me.*

# Dustin

The woods spoke to him, to some quiet part of his soul he wouldn't have known existed if not for it echoing through his bones. It was this way as long as he could remember. Dustin could not bear the four walls of his room or the comfort of his home for very long. So as the sun began to peek over the tops of the tall pine trees that grew near his home, he set out to explore the forest that grew around him for miles.

His house stood beside a dirt road that ran in two directions. To the west, it led to Crow Valley, a small East Texas town built alongside an interstate highway. To the east, it led into a deep wilderness that was made up of deer leases and abandoned cattle ranches. The house, a three bedroom ranch style with a yellow brick exterior, sat on top of a small hill surrounded by about five acres of a green pasture. Dustin's father let some people from town cut and bale the hay it produced in return for a percentage of the sales.

Dustin walked quickly down the dirt road, feeling his feet sink into the thick sand, kicking the occasional rock. After about a quarter mile, the road turned at a ninety degree angle and headed north. At the turn was a driveway with a tiny gravel private road that led to a small mobile home near a deep forest, where Dustin was headed.

It was the first day of summer vacation, and Dustin had decided to explore the woods to the east of his house. He was starting at the property with the mobile home. An older couple, the Carters, bought the land a few years ago with plans to start building a house. They left last summer, but still owned the land. They'd always been nice to Dustin and never cared about him running around in the woods, so long as he didn't leave any trash.

He passed the mobile home and noticed an early model Ford truck parked beside it. Maybe it was the Carters, back from where ever they'd gone. He didn't remember them having a truck, but he hadn't seen them in a year, so they could have bought one. Dustin shrugged his shoulders and continued on.

Every time he stepped into the woods, he felt like he became part of something bigger than himself. Something alive and complex. The bright sunlight faded away as Dustin walked deeper into the dark canopy of trees. Dead, rusty orange pine needles crunched beneath his feet. The smell of rotting wood from fallen trees invaded his nostrils and Dustin breathed deep.

He stopped by the creek that ran through the woods, a narrow brown stream that pooled deeply in some areas and slowed to a trickle in others. This was one of the deeper spots, almost a pond, because of an old beaver dam. The beavers were long gone, and the dam had fallen into severe disrepair. Now it mostly looked like a pile of sticks.

Dustin stood near the dam, counting turtles and keeping an eye on the water moccasin he spotted on the other side of the creek. He searched the ground for some rocks to skip on the water, but couldn't find any. The soothing sound of the water trickling through the woods made him feel at home, and Dustin wondered why anyone would want to live anywhere else.

As he watched a large turtle slowly open and close its mouth, Dustin became aware of something. At first he wasn't exactly sure of what the feeling was, but the hair on his neck stood up and goose bumps appeared on his arms. Some instinct told him to stand still. His first thought was to search the ground for snakes, but he didn't see any. Then he heard the rumble.

Deep and throaty, he knew it was a growl, and it came from behind him. Dustin's hands began shaking and his breathes became shallow. Slowly turning his head, he saw a dark shadow descend the tree behind him. Though he knew he shouldn't, Dustin couldn't help but look. There seemed to be two voices in his head, one screaming to stay completely still and the other screaming to find out what shared these woods with him.

Standing beside the tree was the largest cat he had ever seen. A large, black panther stood staring back at him. His pale yellow eyes flicked side to side quickly, and his nose wiggled slightly as he smelled the air. Dustin could see its muscles rippling in its shoulders and legs. Its yellow eyes watched him intently, waiting for something.

The panther stood there staring for several moments, curious. Dustin's legs began trembling badly and tears fell down his cheeks. He wanted his father to appear and protect him, and he wanted his mother to hold him and tell him that everything would be okay. He felt tiny and alone, certain that he would die.

But the panther simply growled and slowly walked away, following the creek until he was out of sight. The voices inside started arguing again, one screaming to run home and the other telling him to follow the panther. Either way, Dustin's legs felt as heavy as stones, and he couldn't move. He'd always heard of being frozen with fear, and now he was living it.

He wasn't sure how long he stood there, but at some point a mockingbird called out, imitating the roar of the panther. The odd sound brought life back to Dustin's legs, and he lit out for his house, looking back over his shoulder.

His lungs burned as his feet sunk into the sand of the dirt road. When he got back to his house, he stood in the front yard, bent over, hands on his knees. His legs trembled. Beads of sweat had formed on his forehead.

He laid down on the ground, felt the grass against the skin on his arms and legs. The blue sky above him felt endless, especially after being in the woods. He could still see the panther, its yellow eyes and white teeth.

Dustin smiled. The summer was only a day old, and he was already having an adventure.

# Lane

The dreams woke him again. Not the usual ones, filled with broken glass, blood, and fire. This time there were demons. Strange figures with mangled faces, horns, and disgusting, rotting teeth sharp enough to rip through flesh. They crept toward him as he stood on a road that stretched miles in both directions. As they surrounded him, their stench choked him and brought tears to his eyes.

Lane woke before the demons reached him. He looked at the red numbers of the alarm clock by his bed and saw that it was almost noon. His whole life he'd been an early riser, someone who got the job done before others even started. Now he lay in bed, considering going back to sleep. The only thing that stopped him were the demons waiting in his mind.

He went to the kitchen and grabbed a bottle from the top of the fridge. The green linoleum felt cool beneath his feet. He found a plastic cup from the cabinets beside the fridge and filled it with the whiskey. Lane laughed a little, recalling the times he'd given friends grief for drinking in the afternoon.

He opened all the cabinet doors as he sipped, pausing and feeling the burn descend through his throat and into his stomach. His parents had left most of their belongings in the mobile home, so he didn't have to worry about much in way of supplies. There were the usual plates, bowls, and utensils. One cabinet had towels, wash cloths, and pot holders.

The last cabinet Lane opened had bandages and medicine in it. He grabbed a bottle of over-the-counter painkillers and held it in his hand. He shook it lightly and found it to be mostly full. Holding it close to his face, he read that the little white pills shouldn't be combined with alcohol and that taking more than two at a time was dangerous. He held the bottle in his hand for a moment, rotating it slowly with his index finger and thumb. After a while, Lane set it on the kitchen counter and left it there.

He poured more whiskey in the cup and walked to the porch. His father had built it not long after they moved the mobile home onto the property. It wasn't much, only about ten feet by ten feet, but it was enough for a few plastic patio chairs. Lane sat in one and squinted through the late morning sun, listening to the martins and cardinals calling out to one another.

The porch was on the back of the mobile home, overlooking a small field that stretched about fifty yards toward the woods that made up the bulk of his parents' property. There were about fifty acres of pine, oak, and cedar trees that Lane's father had planned to use for deer hunting. If Lane remembered correctly, there was also a creek that flowed through the woods, which emptied into the Trinity River, several miles east of the property.

Lane stared into the woods, thinking about how deep they were. He took a gulp of the whiskey and saw a few dark black grackles fly into the air, startled by a young boy running out of the woods. He was skinny, with shaggy brown hair and long arms. He would probably make a good baseball player one day.

Lane watched him run quickly through the field, stumbling

and looking back toward the woods as if something were following him. Lane searched the tree line, but saw nothing. The boy ran up the gravel drive toward the county road. Lane figured he lived at the house up on the hill. He took another swig of whiskey and decided he'd have to talk with the neighbors. He'd come here for some peace and quiet, and he didn't need some kid disturbing him.

Lane sat in a flimsy plastic chair and continued sipping the whiskey. The sun felt warm and it made him drowsy. He fell asleep and dropped the empty cup, birds chirping all around him.

# Victor

The moon cast a pale blue light over the countryside, making it easy for Victor to finish his task. He parked his car beside the tiny house he shared with his mother and got out. The night seemed alive, and Victor couldn't keep his hands from trembling. He walked to the large barrel he kept about fifty yards from the house. They lived too far out in the country to have garbage service, so they just burned their trash in the barrel.

Victor used the lighter he kept in his pocket to set fire to the trash he'd placed there earlier in the day. He watched as the flames grew into a blaze, his eyes staring into the orange tendrils of energy. He'd always loved to see things burn. Once the fire had grown large enough, Victor began taking his clothes off, piece by piece. As he took them off, he threw them into the fire and watched them burn.

When the fire started dying down, Victor went inside. He paused in the living room and looked at his mother, who was sleeping in a recliner. The television was on, blaring some late night talk show host's tired monologue. He shook his head in disgust and continued to his bedroom.

He showered in the hottest water and scrubbed with soap for twenty minutes. It was important to wash away any trace of what happened. After the shower, he trimmed his nails and then soaked his hands in alcohol. He'd worn gloves, but Victor was thorough and precise.

Victor dressed in light flannel pajamas, turned out the lights, and got into bed. He closed his eyes and pictured the old man, gasping for breath and turning red. In the darkness, Victor smiled and listened to the clock on the wall tick away the seconds. It wouldn't be long until the old man finally paid Victor what he was due. The god of the underneath was so good to him.

# Wendy

The day was nearing its end, but the heat hung in the air like a curtain. Wendy had the air conditioning in the car as cold as it would go, but sweat still beaded on her forehead. Her car was old and probably needed an AC tune-up. She was glad when she parked underneath the large pecan tree that grew beside her house.

As soon as she walked in she could smell Granny's cooking. Wendy inhaled the aroma of pinto beans, cornbread, and roast beef. She hadn't realized until now that she was very hungry. She went to her bedroom and stripped out of her scrubs, which were filthy. As she passed her mirror, she stopped and stared back at herself. Probably too skinny, she thought. She didn't eat as much as she should. She hadn't since she moved back in with Granny.

Her back ached. She stretched and put on a long nightgown. She didn't plan on going out, and they weren't expecting company. After putting her hair in a ponytail, she went to find Granny, who usually sat on the porch while she waited for Wendy to get home.

"Evening, sweetie," Granny said. She sat in her rocking chair near the door, knitting something. Wendy guessed it would eventually become a baby blanket for some young couple at their church. She sat down in the porch swing beside her.

"How was your day, Granny?"

"Good, good. Can't complain." Granny set the knitting down in her lap. "How about yours?"

"Long. You know how it is at the dentist's office, kids spitting on me all day."

"I see."

"Why'd you cook all that food?" Wendy asked. "It's only the two of us."

"I'm just making sure I've got enough in case you ever bring a man home."

Wendy rolled her eyes. "I'm doing fine without a man. We're doing fine."

Granny picked up her knitting and started at it again. Wendy watched her for a while, wondering how the old woman could move her hands so deftly. There had been plenty of times that Wendy had tried to learn, but so far the ability to knit had evaded her.

"I need to call Elaine Phillips," Granny said. "It's been too long since I've talked to her."

Wendy simply nodded. Elaine Phillips had been dead for three years. There was no point in telling Granny this. She'd forget to call anyway.

"Food's probably ready," Granny said as she stood up. "Come help me get it on the table."

Wendy followed her inside. They ate together quietly and then watched television until they both fell asleep. When she woke at a quarter to midnight, she felt grateful and sad at the same time.

# Daryl

Teeth clenched, Daryl listened to all the reasons why he couldn't buy the boat he'd had his eye on for years. His wife listed things that needed to be fixed around the house. She mentioned college money for Dustin. She talked about retirement funds. He knew all these things were important. But he wanted to remind Melissa of all the times they had put off responsible, intelligent purchases in favor of following their hearts. That trip to Puerto Rico when Padre Island would have been fine. The TV with the sixty inch screen. Even Dustin, especially Dustin, was a decision made without thinking of finances.

He stared at Melissa's face as she spoke, wondering where that passion had gone. There were tiny lines appearing in the corners of her eyes and mouth. Some larger ones on her forehead. She was getting older, but he still found her beautiful. But sometime in the past twenty years she had forgotten how to live, and it had sapped the life from her face.

"I get it," he finally said, interrupting Melissa. "You can stop."

"I don't know if I can," she said. "You don't get it."

"I get it." Daryl stood up and walked away from the kitchen table. He stood and stared out the window above the sink. "There's other stuff we can spend the money on. But I told you years ago I was saving for that boat."

"I know."

Daryl turned and felt his face flush. "Then why are you hassling me about this? I work hard. I deserve this."

"Daryl, we can't afford it," Melissa said. "We need to start saving for Dustin's college, and we need to replace the siding on the house."

"I heard you the first time."

"I'm just saying buy a smaller boat." Melissa stood and walked over to him. "I know you had your mind set on a certain boat. But we can't afford that one. I don't want to take away your dream. I just want you to be realistic."

"I'm tired of being realistic," Daryl said. "I want to do something stupid. I want to do this because it will make me feel good, every weekend, for years."

"You can't feel good all the time. You have to make sacrifices."

"I sacrifice all the time!" Daryl yelled. He turned on Melissa, getting in her face. She flinched slightly, which made him even angrier. He'd never touched her in anger once in his life, and here she was acting like a beaten dog.

"Daryl."

"Shut up! Just shut up! I work and provide for you and Dustin! You've never had to have a job. I've always made sure you have enough. Don't talk to me about sacrifice!"

"Stop screaming at me!"

Daryl took a deep breath to begin another round of screaming, but instead he just pushed his way past Melissa. He was tired of her voice, sick of her whining. He went out through the back door, slamming it as hard as he could to help Melissa understand his rage. Once he had his truck started, he roared out of the driveway, slinging gravel and dirt in every direction.

Usually he listened to the old time country music station out of Union City, but today he rode in silence, occasionally screaming out an especially profane curse word. Daryl tried to remember the last time his wife said something other than "no." He took the curves in the road much too fast, even though he wasn't sure where he was going. He just knew he had to get away from Melissa, before he said something he might regret.

When he got to Crow Valley, he just drove up and down the main strip, trying to figure out what he was going to do for a couple hours. In a town this small, there wasn't much in way of distractions, which was why there was such a big problem with teenagers getting drunk and hitting trees with cars. He'd seen the pictures in the paper.

After a while his stomach started growling, and he realized that he needed food. Daryl turned into Shelley's, the local diner. Shelley's specialized in greasy food, the kind that made your arteries clog and your eyelids heavy. It was the type of meal he needed to take his mind off of Melissa.

Once inside, he took a deep breath and smelled fries, waffles, and cigarette smoke. You weren't allowed to smoke in Shelley's anymore, but the scent lingered from years of truck drivers billowing away. The whole diner had a yellow quality to it, whether it was produced by the bad lighting or the heavy grease in the air. Booths lined the walls, with a few tables in the middle, and a counter stood between the seating area and the kitchen. Daryl took a seat at the counter.

A waitress in her late twenties drifted over with a menu. He looked her over and was happy he'd decided to eat at Shelley's. She had blonde hair and blue eyes. Probably as tall as him, she was skinny but still had curves in the right places. She smiled a little when they made eye contact.

"Hey, what can I get you to drink?" she asked, placing the menu in front of him.

"Some sweet tea would be good."

"Alright, I'll be right back."

Daryl watched her walk down the counter and pour the iced tea. He already knew he wanted a hamburger, but he browsed the menu anyway, so the waitress wouldn't catch him staring at her. She came back with a large glass of sweet tea and put it down on a napkin.

"You know what you want?" she asked.

"Yeah, I'll just take a cheeseburger, no onions, with mayo," Daryl said. He folded up the menu and handed it back to her.

"Alright. I'll get your order in. My name is Trisha. If you need anything, just holler at me, okay?"

"Sure thing."

Daryl took a sip of the tea and watched Trisha move from table to table, checking on customers. Her hips swayed as she walked, which Daryl liked. He smelled his burger on the grill, could hear the laughter of all the truckers and teenagers that were eating with him. He'd always liked Shelley's. He watched Trisha laugh as she talked with a table of older women. There was something about that smile. He decided to start eating here more often.

# Melissa

There had always been something about habits and routines that appealed to Melissa. Every morning and night she had her rituals. She enjoyed going to church, because it was the same every time. Sing three hymns, take up the offering, sing another song, then have a sermon, and sing another song. She knew when to stand and when to sit, when to pray and when to be quiet. She liked playing the same Christmas songs while her family unwrapped gifts during the holidays. There was a comfort in those habits and routines.

So now, when she felt so uncomfortable after her conversation with Daryl, she still made supper and set it on the table. Even if it was just her and Dustin. They sat down, said a prayer of thanks for the food, and started eating. She even set a plate for Daryl, even though she was certain he wouldn't be joining them. He wouldn't be home until after she'd gone to bed.

Melissa gritted her teeth to keep the tears from falling. She couldn't tell if they were tears of sadness or anger. Probably a little of both. Daryl was being unreasonable, and she didn't know why. The truth was they couldn't afford the boat. She knew what he was thinking. The money was there in the savings account, so in his mind they had plenty. But Daryl was never very good at planning for the future, and he didn't realize that their credit cards were pretty much maxed out. They had no equity in the house, and the savings were really all they had if some sort of emergency happened. And it was her experience that as soon as you made some huge purchase like a boat, expenses started cropping up left and right.

"Where's Dad?"

"What?"

"Dad." Dustin swallowed some food. "Where's he at?"

"Oh." Melissa took a sip of tea to stall. "He's got some business to handle tonight, so he's not going to make it here."

"Then why'd you set a plate for him?"

"In case somehow he makes it in time."

"Oh."

They were silent for a while, with only the sounds of utensils scraping plates and chewing to fill the air. Melissa chewed angrily. They couldn't even afford the smaller boat in her opinion, but she knew Daryl's mind was set on getting the boat. She was trying to limit the damage.

"What kind of business?" Dustin asked.

"I'm not exactly sure, sweetie." Melissa got up and poured herself some more tea. "But you know, game warden type stuff. I'm sorry, I didn't ask him."

"Oh. Just wondering."

By the end of supper, Melissa had cooled down a little. She and Daryl had been through some serious arguments, though she couldn't remember him screaming in her face before. But he would realize he was being irrational, and she would meet him halfway. They would compromise, like they'd done in the past. She decided to go talk to Sherry Branch, the pastor's wife, who could usually be counted on to give good advice.

Melissa and Dustin washed the dishes together. She rinsed the food off with soap and water, little bubbles filling the air around the sink. Dustin dried with a red dish cloth with white stripes. It reminded her of an apron her grandmother used to wear.

"What did you do today?" she asked. Dustin was drying the last plate and focused on it.

"Went out in the woods down the road," he replied. "Then nothing."

"Be careful out there."

"Are the Carters back?" he asked, putting the plate down.

Melissa took the dish towel from him and dried her hands. "I don't think so. Why?"

"I saw a truck down there."

"Maybe they are."

Dustin shrugged. He needed a haircut, she decided. She loved his hair long, but now he was starting to look unkempt. She reached out and ran her fingers through his hair. He looked annoyed, but didn't stop her.

"You see anything else out there?" Melissa asked.

"Yeah. A panther."

"Really?"

Dustin nodded.

"Hmm. Make sure you tell your father."

"Oh, I will."

He bounced off to his room. Melissa watched him and smiled, saying a quick prayer of thanks for her only son.

# Dustin

The morning couldn't come soon enough. Dustin slept fitfully, waiting for the first tendrils of sunlight to creep through the curtains on his window. Exhaustion would make him succumb for an hour or so, but his excitement would soon wake him again. He trembled in his bed, listening carefully for the first sounds of his parents in the kitchen.

When he heard his father get a coffee mug out of the cabinet, Dustin jumped out of bed and ran to the kitchen. The earthy smell of coffee greeted him as he ran to his father's side. Dustin looked up at him and noticed he looked tired. His face looked droopy and his eyes were red. Dustin tugged on his sleeve.

"Dad?"

"Morning buddy."

"Dad? Can I tell you something?"

"Yeah." His father stared at the coffee as it dripped down into the pot. "Go ahead."

"I think I saw a panther yesterday," Dustin said. He stared up at his father and waited for his reaction.

"What?"

"A panther. Down by the Carter's place. In the woods on their property."

His father's face wrinkled in puzzlement. Dustin wasn't sure what it meant, so he waited for his father to say something. For a long time he just stared at Dustin like he couldn't understand what had been said.

"You saw...a panther?"

"Yup."

"In the woods near here?"

"Yessur," Dustin replied. "Yesterday. I was gonna tell you, but you'd already left and didn't come back until after I was asleep."

His father seemed to regain his composure and poured some coffee into a mug. Dustin watched the steam rise up out of the cup as he did. The scent of the coffee drifted throughout the kitchen, and Dustin breathed deeply. He wished he liked coffee, because it smelled so good. He thought it was very grownup to drink coffee.

"What makes you think you saw a panther?"

"I mean, I did," Dustin replied. "He walked up to me. Growled a little bit. Then walked away."

His father took a sip from the mug. "He just walked right up to you?"

"Yessur."

His father's face wrinkled again, and he set the cup down. "I don't think you saw a panther, buddy."

"Why not?"

"Well, they don't live around here."

"How do you know?" Dustin asked.

"I'm the game warden for Crow County, buddy. It's my job to know stuff like that."

Dustin hung his head and stared at the floor. He felt like his father had reprimanded him, even though he knew it wasn't true. But he was essentially calling Dustin a liar.

"Well, what did I see then?" Dustin asked.

"Maybe it was a bobcat and it just looked dark because of shadows. Was it in a bush?"

"No," Dustin said. "He was right in front of me. Out in the open."

"Hmm…no, buddy, there's no way you saw a panther." His father took a long sip of the coffee. "People say they see them all the time, but it's just rumors. Sometimes your mind plays tricks on you. You probably heard some of those people talking about panthers, and then saw something that made you think it was one."

"I guess."

"Just be careful in those woods, okay? Watch out for wild animals. Keep an eye out for snakes. You remember what I told you?"

"Be careful stepping over logs, 'cause that's where they usually are."

"Right."

"Okay…" Dustin didn't know what to say now and didn't know how to leave. "Dad?"

"Yeah, buddy."

"Umm…never mind."

"Okay."

His father filled up the mug with more coffee and then padded toward the living room to watch the news, his usual routine. Dustin started slinking back to his room, slowly feeling a red rage developing in his chest. The burn moved its way to his cheeks and then his eyes, which began watering. His father called him a liar. Dustin crawled back into bed and pulled the sheets over his head until he was hot and sweaty and the morning was half over and his father was gone.

# Lane

E ven before he fell asleep, Lane knew the dreams would come. He knew they would be waiting for him when he closed his eyes. The darkness in his dream was thick and heavy, but he knew they were there. They were always waiting.

He started shaking, trembling so violently it felt as if his bones would disintegrate into dust. The sweat began trickling down his forehead, then down his back until it snaked down his thighs and calves. He was cold, despite the fact that it was summer. Or was it summer? Perhaps there were no seasons in dreams. Or in hell.

And then they stepped out of the darkness toward him. There were six of them, always six. Their bodies were like men, but their heads were bleached out cow skulls with rotting flesh hanging off of them. They each held torches which burned with a dingy yellow light, slightly tilting them toward him. Lane knew this was a dream, but his heart still beat wildly and he tasted stomach acid at the back of his mouth.

"We have found you." They spoke in unison, making them sound like droning insects. "We will always find you."

Lane started running in the opposite direction. But his steps didn't take him far, and it felt like gravity no longer held as strong a pull on the Earth. He only floated slowly forward with every stride, and when he turned to look back at them, they were following at a stroll. He decided to stop running.

"What do you want?" he asked.

"You."

"Why?" Lane's voice quivered and tears began falling, mingling with the sweat on his face. "Why? You took everything else."

"There is more." Their voices blended together into a whirlwind of hate. "We want more."

Lane collapsed on to the ground, which felt sticky and warm, looking up at the demons. He knew that's what they were, and he screamed as loud as he could out of anger, and fear, and desperation. They laughed and laughed, moving closer and closer until he felt their hot breath on his face. Behind them he saw a bright yellow light, but their hideous faces blocked his view.

Then he woke in a hot sweat, sheets tangled all around him. He could hear the demons laughter ringing in his ears. The moon shone through the curtains, and Lane could see everything in the room clearly. For some reason that frightened him. He got up, went to the kitchen and poured himself a large glass of strong whiskey. There would be no rest without it.

# Victor

The flowerbeds gave off an earthy smell that Victor found appealing. So as he spread the soil around the newly planted periwinkles and daisies, he breathed deeply and smiled. He looked at the black dirt beneath his fingernails and thought of his grandfather the farmer. Victor had followed him around those cotton fields while he worked. They always ended the day with a glass of milk and piece of chocolate cake.

Victor rose from the flowerbed and admired his work. The blue, white, and yellow of the flowers looked nice. He was glad the old man he worked for was gone, because all he ever allowed Victor to plant was monkey grass. Just bland green grass. No different than the rest of his lawn. The old man had no appreciation for beauty. Victor, on the other hand, enjoyed color. He always had, ever since he was a very small child. He would beg his mother for every set of crayons, markers, and colored pencils he saw. Color was life.

He put the spade and half-full bag of soil back in the shed. Looking around, he shook his head in disgust. There was junk everywhere. The old man liked to hold on to everything. When Victor first started working for him, he thought maybe the old man was one of those practical people who thought they might find a use for an old appliance or tool. But soon he realized that the old man just hated the thought of letting go of anything. It was the first of the old man's qualities Victor came to recognize as vile.

He locked the shed up and then walked to his car. After admiring his flowerbed one more time, he glanced at the house and felt his heart beat quicken. It wouldn't be long until the treasure inside belonged to him. Victor would soon be far away from the horrendous heat of the Texas summers, somewhere on an island in the Pacific or the Caribbean or perhaps off the coast of Spain. It didn't matter where, as long as it was an island and the temperature was tropical. But he had to be patient. That is where the typical criminal failed, and Victor was so much more intelligent than a common crook. He was stronger, more fierce. Willing to do anything to get what he wanted. Victor drove away from the old man's house, confident that he was entering the final stretch of his long journey.

# Wendy

The dark sky felt close, and Wendy huddled beneath it. She'd parked her car and laid on the hood staring up at the stars through the windshield. It was so big and made her feel so small, but also safe. Like lying in bed with blankets pulled over your head. She loved it.

After a few more minutes, she grabbed her purse and strolled toward the porch. She took off her shoes and felt the grass tickle the bottoms of her feet. Crickets chirped all around her, so Wendy hummed a song with them as she walked. It was a simple country song she'd heard on the radio on her way home.

"You have a good time?"

Wendy looked up and saw Granny sitting on the porch in her rocker. She was smiling down at Wendy, obviously amused to find her singing tunes to the bugs in the yard. Wendy ascended the stairs and sat down on the porch swing next to Granny.

"It was...okay," Wendy said.

"Oh?"

"Yeah, he was nice. But just...nice. Nothing special."

"You're being picky," Granny said.

Wendy slid her bare feet across the wooden planks of the porch and gently rocked the swing. "No, not too much."

"It's okay. You can afford to be a little picky, with those looks of yours."

"Granny."

Granny giggled, and it made Wendy smile. They sat there in silence for a few minutes listening to the crickets call out to one another. As a child, Wendy used to wish she could understand them. She wanted to hear the love songs they sang.

"Honey, you can't be afraid to let someone get close to you," Granny said. "I know what happened to you was hard. It was wrong. But you have to trust someone again, or you'll miss some beautiful things."

"It's not that." Wendy pulled her legs up to her chest and hugged them. "They think I need to be saved. They think I'm in trouble and that I can't handle being alone and that taking care of you is more than I can handle and all that."

"Do they now?"

"And I don't need that. I'm not looking for some knight in shining armor and all that crap. I'm looking for a friend. A partner. Someone to share my road. And all these guys want to do is rescue the damsel in distress. I know I should probably look past that, because they're probably good men, but I just can't."

Granny reached over and grabbed her hand and squeezed it. "No, I understand honey. A real man doesn't rescue a woman to feel better about himself. A real man knows that a woman is the strongest creature God ever made."

They sat on the porch for a long time, listening to the night while a warm breeze flowed over their skin like honey. Wendy closed her eyes and bit her lip. Despite the beauty and comfort and love surrounding her, she couldn't escape the fact that she was terribly lonely. But giving in to loneliness is what caused the disaster that was her first marriage. She wouldn't do that again.

Maybe she'd never find another man to love. That would be okay. She and Granny got along just fine. Wendy was content to leave her romantic life in God's hands. She leaned into Granny and dozed off with a slight smile on her face.

# Daryl

The trees painted a familiar scene by the road, and Daryl realized they hadn't changed as long as he could remember. He would be forty-five in November, and those trees were older than that. He couldn't remember a time when they didn't line the side of the road like silent sentinels, guarding the road against change. It was like driving through a photograph every day.

He took a left onto the farm-to-market road a few miles outside of town, the same as he done for the last nineteen years. In a few minutes he would make a right onto a dirt road which was only three miles from the dirt road he lived on as a kid. Sometimes, when he was just sitting around at work, he would imagine his footsteps falling on every square inch of this county. When he was younger, he thought it was a good thing, an admirable thing. Now he was beginning to think it was foolish.

He knew when he turned off that dirt road and parked his car, he would go into his house and change his clothes. He and

Melissa would exchange pleasantries that had become so rote he could scarcely remember what they'd said to each other afterward. He would grab some sort of snack from the kitchen. Chips, pickles, or pretzels. Maybe one of Melissa's yogurt cups if he was trying to be healthy. Then he'd sit and watch TV, maybe go outside and work in the yard until dinner. After dinner he'd watch more TV, or read a magazine. Then he would go to bed, and in the morning would begin the routine again. Making the same turns, passing the same trees which never seemed to change.

Daryl had decided to become a game warden when he was young. Probably the beginning of high school if he remembered correctly. He always loved hunting. His father took him all the time as a kid, and there was no part of it he didn't like. Whenever he got free time, he was out hunting and fishing. He could still feel the adrenaline rush of his first deer, how it felt to pull the trigger and know the shot was true. The smell of the blood as his father showed him how to dress it. The more time he spent hunting and fishing, the more he felt a connection to the animals and the environment which they inhabited.

As he matured, he realized he wanted to give something back to the woods. He wanted to show the men who'd taught him how to hunt and fish he understood what they had told him about respecting the game he hunted, and the weapons he used, and how hunting and fishing were a tradition passed down from ancestors so far back he couldn't even fathom the generations.

After high school, he went to college at Givens University and majored in Wildlife Management. He then bounced around Texas, participating in internships and low level jobs at state and national parks until he passed his exams and went through training at the academy. And then, as if by fate, when he was eligible to become a game warden, a job opened up in Crow County, and he got it. He moved back, met Melissa, had Dustin, and had been doing the same thing for almost two decades.

Daryl sighed as he made the right turn onto the dirt road and felt the mix of gravel, sand, and clay crunch beneath his truck's tires.

He slowly rolled along the road, again looking at trees that had never changed as long as he could remember. How was it possible that a storm hadn't caused one of them to fall over at some point in the last ten years?

As his truck moved down the road, Daryl began to feel a tightness in his chest that he couldn't explain. If he didn't know any better, he would have thought he was having a heart attack. But there was no shortness of breath or pain in his right arm. He could actually feel his heartbeat, and it was very normal. This tightness was like a monster gripping his heart and squeezing it. Daryl didn't like the way it felt. He reached up and massaged his chest muscles with the knuckles of his fingers until the feeling went away. Maybe he was just dehydrated.

Daryl could see his home down the road. It was the last step in his autopilot ride home, and as he saw it growing larger in his windshield, he felt the tightness return. It gripped his whole body as he moved closer. Massaging his chest didn't help this time. And then he thought of going inside, and doing the same routine one more time. The tightness increased, and he felt like his heart was going to explode. He felt like he would die if he went inside for another meal, another routine evening in his home. It felt like there was some pressure inside every vein and artery in his body, and going inside would be the last straw. It would cause him to explode. Yes, he was certain he would die.

So Daryl made the simple decision to keep driving. He passed his home, and then passed the Carters' old place. He drove with no direction and no aim. After a few minutes, the tightness began fading away, which made him feel relieved. He rolled the windows of his truck down and let the country air fill the cab. The dust and fresh cut hay and honeysuckle combined into an aroma he'd known all his life but was just beginning to appreciate. He turned up his radio and listened to the music like a teenager, singing along to the words with the abandon that only comes with innocence. All he needed was a glass of lemonade and maybe a cigarette, an old habit he kicked many years ago.

31

After about an hour, Daryl didn't feel like he would die anymore. He drove home and actually felt good by the time he parked his car in the drive. He made some excuse about work to Melissa, who didn't question him. She didn't have a reason to, and it was likely that she barely even heard him. But it was okay, at least for today. He'd relieved the tightness with only a ride through the country with his windows down. When the day was over and Daryl laid in bed, staring up at the ceiling in the dark, he remembered the way the music and the air and the honeysuckle had brought him back to life.

# Melissa

On Saturday mornings, Melissa headed to Cross Roads Baptist Church to attend a women's bible study. Sometimes she looked forward to it. Other times it was a chore to be completed. When she didn't feel like going, she considered staying home, but being absent made her feel guilty. She didn't think God cared whether she missed bible study, but she knew it would result in a round of phone calls from the women at church asking why she hadn't shown up.

So now she sat listening to the other women talk about what God was doing in their lives. Melissa kept quiet during this part of the meeting. She'd never been one to share personal details. After everyone had said their piece, they started reading from a workbook written by a confident looking woman in her forties. Melissa liked it when it was her turn to read out loud. She'd always been good at that, ever since elementary school, when the teacher would ask her to read books to the class on Friday afternoons.

Afterwards, Melissa approached Sherry Branch and asked to speak with her privately. Sherry led the bible study and was always very enthusiastic. Melissa mostly liked her, and she wasn't afraid to admit to herself that a lot of that feeling had to do with Sherry's appearance. She didn't wear hip clothes and have a perfect complexion. Her hair wasn't styled every time she went out. She was almost the opposite of the workbook author, who would have intimidated Melissa if they ever met.

They went into one of the small Sunday school rooms to talk. Its walls were filled with old posters of Jesus, the Ten Commandments, and children reading bibles. Sherry and Melissa sat down beside each other on metal folding chairs. The metal was cold on the parts of her bare legs that weren't covered by her skirt, which was kind of short, so she was sure it had given some of the more catty women something to talk about after the meeting.

"Thanks for talking with me," Melissa said.

Sherry reached over and put a hand on top of Melissa's. "Anytime, honey. That's what I'm here for."

Melissa didn't like that Sherry called her "honey." They were almost the same age. But she decided to ignore it and move on. She needed someone to talk to, someone who gave advice all the time.

"Me and Daryl are having problems," Melissa said. "I mean, not serious problems. But things aren't good. We're arguing a lot."

"Okay." Sherry looked at her with concern.

"Nothing big has happened. Nobody cheated on anybody." Melissa laughed to lighten the mood, but Sherry didn't even smile. "Nothing major. It's just money stuff."

"Hmm. That happens a lot," Sherry said. "Most of the couples we talk to. Money causes a lot of problems."

"Well, Daryl just has it in his head that he wants to buy a boat," Melissa said. "And we can sort of afford it, but not really. You know what I mean?"

"Oh, I do, honey."

"We've got a little money saved up, but there's other things that need attention. And we need to save up for Dustin's college. We don't have time to go anywhere as it is right now, so I know we won't have time for using that boat."

"I know what you mean," Sherry said. "Last year Kenneth had to buy a new lawnmower, even though the one we had was running just fine. But he said it had two blades, or something like that. I don't know. Point is, he wanted it, wouldn't back down, started saying he worked hard, you know. All that kind of stuff. Seems like these men just get stubborn from time to time, feel the need to buy something manly to make'em feel better."

"I guess."

"He's probably just having a mini mid-life crisis. Maybe try and get him to take a vacation he's been wanting to go on for a while. Or a new gun maybe."

"Yeah, I was thinking about that. Or a less expensive boat."

Sherry patted her on the leg enthusiastically. "There you go! Just remember, all men go through stuff like this. Try and help him make good decisions. But remember to be submissive and let him lead you. And I've found it helps to make sure you're being the best woman you can be for him."

"What do you mean?"

"Well, honey, you know. Make sure you put on makeup, wear your nice clothes, keep the house clean. Maybe make his favorite food a few times over the next couple weeks. Stay skinny for him." At this Sherry leaned forward and touched Melissa's hand. "Not that you need to lose much weight, honey, but we could all stand to be a little healthier."

"Okay."

Sherry stood up gracefully and with a flourish. As she did Melissa caught a whiff of her rose scented perfume. It made her want to smell like a flower, too. Melissa stood because it seemed like Sherry expected her to.

"Does that help you?" Sherry asked.

"Yes, thank you. Thanks so much for listening."

"Anytime, honey, anytime. And if you need to talk again, you've got my phone number. Just call me whenever."

"Thank you Sherry."

Sherry smiled and hugged Melissa. She felt skinny, and Melissa was jealous, but only a little. Sherry wasn't much thinner than she was. But Melissa could lose a little weight. She went home and really didn't think about the bible study at all. She did look up some healthy recipes and exercise routines, though.

# Dustin

The forest swayed with the warm wind that was sweeping more hot air in from the west. At times it sounded like every tree was creaking and aching and threatening to fall. Usually when the fronts came through they brought rain with them. But not this time. Dustin kicked at the pine needles at his feet and surveyed the area.

He tried hard to think about where he would be if he were a panther. The creek was a good place to start. It was the closest source of water. There was a pond, deeper into the woods, though. Maybe the panther was there. Then again, maybe it was long gone, traveling east into Louisiana.

Dustin ducked under a fallen sapling and got a mouthful of spider web. He pried it away from his face and moved on, following an old cow trail that led toward the creek. Following the creek into the woods didn't seem like a bad plan. With its soft muddy banks, it'd be the best place to find tracks.

Dustin took the trail around a large oak tree with blackberry bushes growing wild around its trunk. As he passed he heard a noise near the bushes and looked down to find a baby hog rooting around in the soil. His heart started beating hard. Dustin was young, but he was smart enough to know that the hog's mother would be somewhere near. He tried to move back slowly and not scare the baby hog, but after one step he heard the snort he'd hoped wouldn't come.

He turned his head and saw the mama hog about ten feet away, standing still and looking at him. She just stared, like she was trying to figure out if he was a threat. Dustin didn't want to wait around for her decision. He took a sideways step, trying to get out from in between the mama hog and her baby. But his movement spurred her to action, and she squealed out loud. That got the baby hog's attention, and he let out a squeal, too. Dustin looked at her angry, beady eyes set into her coarse black hair and was sure they were the last thing he would see before she tore into him.

But just as the mama hog took a step forward, a thunderous explosion rang out to Dustin's left. It stopped the mama hog in her tracks and sent the baby hog scurrying away. Dustin looked over where it came from and saw a lanky man in his late twenties holding a large rifle. The man fired the gun into the air again, and even though Dustin saw him do it, the sound still made him jump. And it sent the mama hog running after the baby. Dustin watched her run away. He let out a long breath when she disappeared.

The lanky man sauntered over to him slowly. "Saw those hogs in my pasture this morning. Watched'em go into the woods. Then about an hour later you came along, followed'em right in. Figured I come down here and let you know."

"Thanks."

The lanky man stuck his hand out. "Lane."

"Dustin." He shook Lane's hand limply, because he was still in shock about what had just happened.

"How old are you, Dustin?"

"Twelve."

Lane sat down on a large fallen tree near them. He held the

rifle by the barrel with the butt on the ground. He regarded Dustin for a second.

"Well, I figure that's old enough to know about trespassing," Lane said. "You know you're on my land, right?"

"Yessur."

Lane smiled. "Least you're honest."

Dustin didn't say anything. A bird flitted from one branch to another and it caught his eye. He wished he had wings and could fly away from problems because he would fly away in moments like these.

"You normally just go running around on other people's land?"

"No sir," Dustin replied. "But the people that used to live here didn't mind."

"The people here before?"

"The Carters."

"That'd be my parents," Lane said. "They're now in Florida. Or Georgia. Somewhere in that area. Hard to keep up with'em since their house has wheels, you know?"

Dustin nodded.

"So they didn't care about you being out here?"

"No, sir. They said long as I didn't throw any trash on the ground, I could explore down here much as I wanted."

Lane pulled out a pack of cigarettes and lit one. The acrid smell of smoke drifted over to Dustin and made him want to cough, but he held back. He didn't want Lane to think he was a sissy.

"Well, I suppose if my parents were okay with you running around out here, I am, too," Lane said. "Just pay attention. Watch out for hogs."

"More than hogs out here," Dustin said. He took a few steps toward Lane and tried to hide his excitement.

"Like what?"

"I saw a panther a few days ago," Dustin said. "Not far from right here."

"How far away from it were you?"

39

"About as far apart as me and you right now."

"Huh," Lane said. "He just walked right up to you?"

Dustin nodded. "Just growled a little and walked away."

"Ain't that something."

"You believe me?" Dustin asked.

"Well, I ain't known you long, but you don't seem like a liar. And I don't see how lying to me about a panther helps you any. So yeah, I believe you."

Dustin walked over and sat down beside Lane on the log. "I'm gonna find him. I want to see him again."

Lane didn't say anything, only raised his eyebrows a little like he was surprised. He stubbed the cigarette out on the log, spit on the end up it and threw it on the ground. Dustin felt awkward with the silence, but tried not to show it.

"You go to church?" Lane asked.

"Yeah, at Cross Roads Baptist Church. Few miles away from here."

"What time does service start on Sunday?"

# Lane

"Don't leave here without knowing Jesus Christ as your personal Savior! You could die this very day! Think on it, congregation. How many stories have you heard of normal, healthy people dropping dead without warning? How many young lives have been lost in tragic car accidents?"

The pastor thundered away at the pulpit, shouting and pleading, begging for the lost to be saved. It was a familiar theme. Lane had grown up listening to it, had slowly stopped hearing it, and then stopped going to church altogether. He didn't really want to hear it anymore. Hadn't cared for it since he found out that Christie was gone. But the liquor had stopped chasing away the demons, and he was desperate.

"What if the Lord Jesus Christ came back this very hour? Would you be caught up with the rest of the saints, in the twinkling of an eye?" the pastor continued. "Would your name be found in the Lamb's book of life? Or when you stand before God, will he say 'depart from me ye worker of iniquity, I know you not'? Friends, don't tarry. Don't take God's mercy and patience for granted. Invite Jesus Christ, the Lamb slain for your sins, into your heart this very day, this very hour, this very minute!"

Lane could see the kid from yesterday sitting a few pews ahead of him. He watched him fidget and lean on his mother's arm, eager to escape the stillness of church for the wild openness of the woods on Lane's property. Lane remembered being the same way at his age. The church he went to as a kid was a lot bigger, though. There were only about eighty people here, according to his estimate.

The pastor kept going with his hell-fire and brimstone, but Lane tuned him out. His eyes wandered over the church, taking in the people and the building. The white paint of the walls was flaking off and falling onto the brown carpet. It made him think of Jesus calling the Pharisees whitewashed tombs with rotting bones inside.

He noticed a woman one pew ahead of him and to the left looking at him. She had blonde hair and large blue eyes. Lane figured she was about his age. He acted like he didn't notice her staring but watched her out of the corner of his eye. She didn't try to hide her gaze or pretend like she was looking at anyone else. So he turned and made eye contact with her, thinking she would turn away. But she didn't. She looked right back at him and smiled. After a few moments, she turned her attention back to the pastor.

"I'm going to ask you to bow your head," the pastor said. "We're going to play a song, and if the Holy Spirit is leaning on your heart, won't you make a decision today and follow Jesus? I'll pray with you, and you can be sure of your place in heaven today. Jesus is knocking on your heart's door. Won't you let him in? Let's pray."

The pastor bowed his head and so did everybody else. Lane kept his head up and watched everyone else. The blonde in the pew ahead of him glanced back and made eye contact again. This time Lane smiled at her, probably the first smile to cross his face in a long time. She laughed and then bowed her head.

The song was played and the pastor prayed a long and elaborate prayer in which he repeated himself often. Lane knew the drill. There'd be weeping sinners on their knees and one more verse by the song leader and then a line at the exit with the pastor waiting to shake his hand. Lane wasn't interested in being social, so he quietly slid out of the pew and left the church.

# Wendy

endy followed the lanky stranger out of the church. She
wasn't sure what she was going to say, but she knew she
wanted to talk to him. The sun was already shining down
hard, and the heat hit her hard as she walked quickly to
catch up with him. Her heels sunk into the grassy area the church
used as a parking lot.

"Hey!" Wendy called out. The man had reached his truck and
was opening the door. He stopped when he heard her and just stared
as she approached.

"Hey."

"What's your name?" Wendy asked. She stood in front of
him, looking up at his face. It looked like it hadn't been shaved in a
couple of days.

"Lane."

"I'm Wendy."

He stuck out his hand, and she took it. His palms had

callouses in places but were soft in others. She worried because the heat might have made her hand sweaty.

"What can I do for you, Wendy?"

"Just wanted to introduce myself. Never seen you in church before. Trying to be friendly."

"Oh." He leaned up against his truck and stuck his hands in his pockets. He was wearing a red plaid button-up with faded blue jeans, and Wendy thought he looked very plain. But she liked it.

"Are you new to the area?" Wendy asked. "It's a small town. I've never seen you before."

"Been here a few weeks. You'd probably be familiar with my parents, though. The Carters. They lived down the road from here."

"I remember them." Wendy leaned against the truck beside him. She could feel the hot metal against her back. "Are you gonna come back?"

"To church?"

"Yeah."

"Don't know. I don't care much for it."

"Then why'd you come today?" Wendy asked.

"Seemed like a good idea at the time."

Wendy didn't understand what that meant. But she didn't ask. She turned her head and looked up at Lane. He was taller than she realized.

"We've got a group for people our age," she said. "Meets on Wednesday nights at seven. You should come."

"Why would I wanna do that?" Lane smiled. "I just told you I don't like church."

"You could come for the company."

He smiled again. "Maybe I'll be there."

"I don't care for half-hearted men."

Lane chuckled. "I'll be there ten minutes early, then."

"Good."

They stood there for a few moments, looking at each other awkwardly. It made Wendy think of being a teenager again. Lane took a baseball cap out of the cab and put it on.

"I should get going," Lane said. "Don't wanna hold you up any longer."

"It's okay. I don't have anywhere to be." Wendy could tell he was nervous, itching to leave.

"No, I should go," he replied. "I'll see you on Wednesday."

"Okay."

Lane got in his truck and drove away. Wendy waited until he was out of sight before she went back inside the church, where things were just beginning to wind down. She quickly said a prayer for Lane, nothing specific because she didn't know him well. Hopefully he'd come back. She thought Granny would like him.

# Daryl

The air was heavy and humid. The smell of the syrup plant just up the highway hovered over the entire town. Daryl looked through the windows of Shelley's, trying to see if the waitress was there. Trisha. He said the name out loud. After a while, he got hungry, so he went inside. He took a seat at the counter and hoped that Trisha would show up.

Then he saw her bringing food to some truckers in a booth. He looked over the menu while he waited for her to come over. Shelley's was busy, which was unusual for a weeknight. Daryl studied the menu like it was complicated. Trisha came walking over, her hips moving back and forth slowly, hypnotizing him.

"Hey," she said. "Back again, huh?"

"Yes, ma'am."

"You're here about as much as me."

"Well, food's good. Company's good. Can't complain."

"You want the same thing?" Trisha asked.

"Yeah, let's go with that."

"Alright. You know the drill."

Trisha took his menu and put in his order. She walked to the far end of the counter and began rolling silverware into napkins. At first Daryl was disappointed she moved so far away from him. But then he noticed she was looking up at him with those big blue eyes, every now and then brushing her hair behind her ear. She noticed him watching her and she smiled.

A few minutes later another waitress brought over his hamburger. Daryl ate slow, watching the crowd move out the door with expectation. When the diner was slow, Trisha would have more time to talk. She usually talked to him. So he lingered over his fries, waiting for her to come over.

After a while, only Daryl and an older couple were left in Shelley's. Trisha kept finding reasons to stand near him, talking about little things that didn't matter. He ordered pie and coffee, which gave him a reason to stay longer.

"How big of a bill you gonna run up?" Trisha asked.

"What?"

"Nothing. I like seeing how much my conversation is worth in dollars."

Daryl felt his face blush a little. "Well, it's worth more than a greasy hamburger and a piece of pie."

"I don't know if that's a compliment or not."

Daryl didn't know what to say, so he just smiled. Trisha smiled back, though, and it made him feel better. She did that thing where she tucked her hair behind her ear. Daryl liked when she did that.

"Well, I guess I'd better be getting home." Daryl got up and left a ten dollar bill on the counter. "I'll see you around."

"I'm working Friday night."

Daryl stopped and turned around. "What?"

"I don't work again until Friday night," Trisha said. "Just thought you'd like to know."

Trisha was folding napkins again, her head down and focused.

She glanced up at him shyly and blinked a few times. Daryl swallowed and looked at her. Again, he didn't know what to say.

"Okay," he finally replied. "I'll see you around."

Daryl put his hands in his pockets and turned to go. He tried not to slouch, squaring back his shoulders and straightening his spine, aware that Trisha might be watching him walk away. He wanted to look confident and young. At the door he turned and waved back at Trisha, then got in his truck and went home.

# Melissa

She'd gotten into the habit of setting a plate for Daryl, even though she knew he wasn't going to show up. A part of her felt like it would make Dustin feel better, but she knew the boy wasn't stupid. He needed his father at home, not just an empty spot at the table. So as she and Dustin sat eating chicken and dumplings, one of Daryl's favorite meals, Melissa stared at the empty seat where her husband usually sat. She got angrier the longer she looked at it.

After they finished eating, she asked Dustin to wash the dishes and clean up the kitchen. He groaned a little but got on the job like a good boy should. Melissa went out on the porch and called Daryl on his cell phone. It rang and rang but he never picked up. After trying three times, she gave up and went back inside. Dustin was still busy in the kitchen, amusing himself by blowing tiny bubbles with the dish detergent.

Melissa went to her bedroom, locked the door and fought the urge to cry. For years her husband had loved her and now it seemed like he didn't. Did that love go away over night? Or had it faded gradually and she just hadn't noticed? Whatever the case, Daryl didn't want to come home. Didn't want to see her or his son more than he had to.

Maybe Sherry was right. This was just a phase Daryl was going through, and soon enough he'd be back to his regular self, eating supper and telling his dumb stories that Dustin found so interesting. Maybe Daryl was just feeling trapped, something she understood. There were times she wanted to jump in her car and drive into the sunset, leaving the mortgage payments and dentist appointments and parent-teacher meetings behind forever. But she didn't, because she knew it was just emotions, and she would regret leaving.

So Melissa decided to keep on making their home a place Daryl wanted to be. She'd keep making his favorite meals and let him know what time supper would be. She'd keep the house extra clean. She stood up in front of her mirror and looked at herself. She wasn't fat, but she could stand to lose a few pounds. How many times had she told herself that?

Melissa changed clothes and put on sneakers, then told Dustin she was going for a walk. She walked a mile on the sandy dirt road that ran by their house, swatting mosquitoes the whole way. When she got home, she went to her bedroom and did sit-ups until her stomach hurt. After taking a shower, she looked up diets online that were supposed to help you lose weight fast. Around ten o'clock she told Dustin goodnight and crawled into bed by herself. She laid awake in the dark until Daryl got home about thirty minutes later. When he got into bed, she pretended she was asleep.

# Dustin

Breakfast was beginning to be the only meal his father was around for anymore. Dustin knew it was the only time he'd really have to corner his father about the panther. He knew that if the two of them went and scouted the woods for the panther, they'd find it. No doubt. His dad was the game warden. He did stuff like this for a living.

Dustin simultaneously watched his father and the clock, trying to get up the courage to say something. Daryl sat sipping coffee, reading the weekly newspaper and not saying much. His mother had finished her eggs and biscuits quickly, then headed out to the front porch to drink her coffee and read a little. She'd been doing that more lately.

"Dad?"

Daryl looked up from the newspaper. Dustin choked a little on his own spit because he was so nervous. But he plowed ahead.

"I was wondering if on one of your days off me and you

could look around for that panther," Dustin said. "Just for a little bit. I think if you helped me we could find it."

Daryl stared at him for a second and then smiled. "Buddy, it's alright if you wanna run around the woods looking for your panther. But I don't think it's out there. I mean, nothing wrong with spending time in the woods. I love it, and I'm glad you do, too. But you're out there looking for a ghost that don't exist."

"But I saw it."

"I don't know, buddy," Daryl said. "It'd be real strange for a panther to live in these woods. It's mostly legends and folk tales from people around here. Maybe you just saw a big cat."

Dustin felt his face burn with a mixture of embarrassment and anger. He mumbled a weak "okay" and then pushed his eggs around a little before leaving the table. He went to his room and put on his jeans and shoes. Then he found the coffee can he used as a bank and emptied the contents on to his bed. He counted out a few dollars and then put the rest back in the can. After filling his backpack with a knife, some snacks, and a bottle of water, he went to the front porch to find his mother.

Dustin handed her the money. "Is this enough to buy a disposable camera?"

"Yes." Melissa looked at the money and then back at Dustin. "What do you need one for?"

"I just wanna take pictures of stuff I see in the woods," Dustin replied. "So I can show everybody what I find."

Melissa smiled and put the money down on the table beside her. "I'll pick one up next time I go to the store. And if it's not enough, I'll cover the rest, okay sweetie?"

"Thanks, mom."

Dustin jumped off the porch and started walking down the road to the Carter's place. Lane's place. On the way, he found a large branch, almost as tall as him, lying on the side of the road. It looked like it was from a crepe myrtle tree. He picked it up and used it as a walking stick. It'd come in handy if he came across anymore hogs. Or the panther.

He didn't care what his dad said. The panther was real because Dustin had seen him. He'd read stories about people who'd seen God. Even one boy from Texas who'd died and gone to heaven where he met Jesus. Dustin had never seen God or Jesus, but he believed all those stories.

Lane believed him. It bothered him that a stranger trusted him more than his own father. Dustin sighed and kicked a rock. He just needed to get a picture of the panther. Then he would show it to everyone, and his dad would believe, too.

# Lane

L ane waited outside the church until almost seven o'clock. He
didn't want to go in any earlier and have to make small-talk.
When he couldn't wait any longer, he drifted in the front door,
avoided eye contact, and looked for Wendy, the reason he was
here. There were less people than on Sunday, which didn't surprise
him.

He didn't find Wendy. She found him. Lane felt someone
touch his arm and turned to see her looking up at him. Her eyes were
a deep blue and it stopped him for a moment. He hadn't cared about
a woman in years, and yet, he felt the seed of something growing
inside his heart.

"Hey," she said. "Glad you could make it."

"Happy to be here."

"No, you're not. But I appreciate you lying. Especially in
church."

Wendy took him by the arm and led him through a hallway

filled with art made by children. They went into a room decorated with flowery wallpaper and purple carpet. About a dozen metal folding chairs were arranged in a circle, about half of them filled with women whose age ranged from twenty to forty. Lane realized he was probably going to be the only male in attendance.

Wendy introduced him to everyone, though Lane quickly forgot all their names. He felt uncomfortable and began watching the clock on the wall, silently urging it to reach eight o'clock as fast as it could. The women were going through some sort of workbook that Lane didn't have. Wendy moved her chair close to him and tried to let him follow along with hers, but he wasn't really interested.

After about an hour of talking about the Bible, the workbook, and their feelings, the meeting ended. All the women thanked him for attending and asked him to come back. Lane smiled and was polite, but the idea of returning didn't appeal to him at all. Opening up to a room full of women didn't sound like fun.

He and Wendy walked out to her car, though it took a while because people kept coming up to her, saying hello, asking to be introduced to Lane. He could tell she was just as embarrassed as he was and only wanted to make it out to the parking lot. When they were finally able to get to her car, a black compact sedan from Japan that looked like it'd seen better days, Wendy sat in the driver's seat and looked up at him.

"Thanks again for coming," she said. "I know you really didn't want to."

Lane put one hand on the roof of the car and leaned against it. "It was okay. I'm glad you invited me."

"There you go lying again."

Lane laughed a little. He didn't know what he was doing here with this girl. He knew this was flirting and it made him feel guilty. But he was already falling, he knew it. He'd felt this way before. Already he was noticing the details that made up Wendy. The small wrinkles beside her eyes. The pitch of her laugh. The light freckles on her cheeks. He'd come to Crow Valley for silence, for the loneliness. Not to find a girl.

"Well...," Lane started. But he couldn't finish the sentence.

"We can't stand here like this forever," Wendy said. She looked up at him earnestly.

"What?"

"You need to ask for my number, or to see me again. Unless you wanna keep coming back to church. Which you said you don't like."

"Oh."

Wendy grabbed a small piece of paper from her console and handed it to him. "It's my number."

"Okay."

"Just wanna make sure things keep moving along here," Wendy said. "Okay?"

"Yeah. I was gonna ask."

"I know you were."

"Thanks."

Wendy smiled up at him, and Lane felt his heart leap in his chest. It was something he hadn't felt in years, and it surprised him, because he was certain it had died years ago. This woman, with her eyes, with her smile, saw him when he stumbled into her church looking for answers.

"I'll talk to you later, right?" Wendy asked.

"Yes, ma'am."

Wendy shut her door. Lane tapped the roof twice and started walking away. Before he was more than a few steps away, though, he heard a loud clicking. He turned and looked at Wendy, turning her key again, which caused more clicking. She got out and popped the hood. Lane walked over and stood beside her.

"Car trouble?" he asked.

"You like pointing out the obvious?"

Lane smirked at her and just watched. Wendy propped the hood open and began tugging on the battery cables. She pulled a pocket knife out of her purse, used it to unscrew the cables, and then scraped the terminals clean.

"Looks like you've done this before," Lane said.

"Few times."

Wendy reconnected the cables and then got back in the car. The engine turned over a couple times before it finally started. Lane shut the hood and walked over to her door again. He looked down at Wendy and smiled. Her face was a little red, like she was embarrassed.

"I think your car could use a little work," he said.

"Yeah, but it's a good car."

"You're right. Good model, always liked these. But it still needs some work. You got some hoses in bad shape, probably need new battery cables. Your belt needs changing."

"You know about cars?"

"I know a little," Lane said. "That's just some stuff I saw."

"Well, I kind of have a philosophy of waiting until it breaks before I fix it. And that philosophy is mostly influenced by my lack of funds. You know?"

Lane smiled. "I do."

"So you'll call me, right?"

"What if I come over. Work on your car." It was a question, but Lane said it more like a statement. Wendy didn't answer, just looked at him a little confused. "It'll save you on the labor, you can just pay for the parts. That fit your budget?"

"I guess so," Wendy said. "I don't want to impose on you, though."

"No trouble. I've got plenty of time, I like doing the work. Give me something to do."

"Something to do?"

"Yeah, keep my hands busy," Lane said.

"Speaking of which, I've been meaning to ask where you work."

Lane looked down and kicked at the gravel. "That's a first date question, ain't it? Hate to ruin our evening before it gets started."

Wendy put both hands on the steering wheel and looked up at him again, smiling brightly. Those eyes. That smile. For a moment, he imagined holding her while she looked up at him like that. Then the feeling was gone, buried under an avalanche of guilt.

"Alright, then," Wendy said. "How about this? You come over on Saturday to work on the car, afterwards I'll feed you. We'll kill two birds with one stone. Sound good?"

"Sounds good." And then, because he couldn't help himself, he reached down and put his hand on top of hers as she held the steering wheel. "I'll call you Friday for directions. What time?"

"You're working for free," Wendy said. "I'm on your schedule."

"Eight o'clock work?"

"Can't wait."

Wendy smiled. Lane closed her door and walked to his truck. He watched her drive away, hoping her car would hold up until Saturday. It was in bad shape, one of the worst he'd seen. As he started up his truck he laughed at the thought of being on a date. Of being alone with a woman again. He needed a drink.

# Victor

The knock on the door didn't surprise him. He'd been waiting for it, anticipating it, yearning for it, aching for the time to come. It needed to happen, needed to happen. Victor had spent days looking out the window, looking for them, waiting for them. Cursing them. Redneck bumpkin police have no idea how to process a missing-persons case.

Two meat-head state troopers on his porch, one of them banging his fat hands on Victor's door. Overweight, unkempt, one of them hadn't shaved. Victor sighed because he knew this would be easy, and he wanted it to be hard, wanted it to be difficult. But it wouldn't be. He waited some more, waited. Waited. Then opened the door.

"Can I help you?" Victor asked. He looked them in the eye, confident. One with brown hair in a crew cut, named Larsen. One with black hair, Hispanic, named Rodriguez. Larsen was fatter, probably in charge. Probably.

"We're looking for Victor Matthews," Larsen said. "Would that be you, sir?"

"Yes, sir. What can I do for you?"

"We just need to ask you a few questions. You mind if we come inside?"

Victor smiled kindly, didn't lose eye contact. "I'd rather we speak on the porch. My mother is ill. I don't want to disturb her. Would that be alright?"

Quick glance between the fat cops, then a slight nod. Victor tried not to smile, didn't want them to know. Had to wait. Always waiting. He stepped out onto the porch and shut the door behind him.

"Mr. Matthews, you work for Charles Kilibrew, correct?"

"Yes."

"When was the last time you saw him?" Larsen asked.

Victor paused for a moment, wrinkled his forehead briefly. "Last Thursday. I mowed his yard. Usually I do it on Fridays, every Friday, but last week I needed Friday off to take my mother to Dallas for a doctor's appointment."

"And you haven't talked to him since?"

"No, but that's not unusual," Victor said. "All of my work at Mr. Kilibrew's is very routine. I've worked for him for years, so I rarely need any instruction. We speak once a week, sometimes every two weeks."

Both troopers nodded and scribbled in small notepads. Victor watched them and made his face look concerned. Look concerned. Care. Act like you care.

"Did he say he was leaving, going anywhere?" Larsen asked.

"No, Mr. Kilibrew rarely left his home. That was part of my job. Running errands for him. He usually only went to his medical appointments."

The troopers nodded again. Victor pretended to care again.

"Is something wrong?" Victor asked. He figured it was time. He'd waited long enough. Always waiting. Wait. Wait. Wait.

"Mr. Kilibrew hasn't shown up to two medical

61

appointments," Larsen said. "His doctor became concerned and asked the authorities to stop by his home to see if everything was okay. There was no answer, but Mr. Kilibrew's vehicle was still home. We're trying to locate Mr. Kilibrew now."

Victor fought to keep from smiling. Dr. Henderson, always sticking his nose into others' affairs. Always. He knew it would be Henderson who would notice the old man's absence, and Henderson who would call the cops. People always behaved the way he predicted. They always behaved true to their nature. They were just waiting to be themselves. Waiting to be themselves always. Waiting.

"That's terrible," Victor said. "I didn't realize."

"Did you see anything around the house lately that would make you think he was leaving? Going somewhere? Airline tickets, cruise trip? Something like that?"

Victor looked at the ground for a moment and tried to look embarrassed. "I'm typically not allowed in the house. Sometimes I was let into the foyer."

The troopers glanced at each other and looked surprised. Victor breathed a little deeper, holding back the smile. Wait to smile. Wait for later. Wait. Cops listening to the story, buying it. Wait for it.

"Mr. Kilibrew was very private," Victor said.

"I see."

Victor looked at them expectantly, ready to answer any other questions. They studied their notepads, making sure they asked all their questions. Victor waited. Always waiting. They asked him a few more questions, mostly about what the old man had been doing lately. But Victor had the distinct feeling that these questions were just filler, inquiries that really didn't matter.

"If you hear from Mr. Kilibrew, give us a call," Larsen said, handing him a business card.

"I definitely will. Please let me know if you find out anything."

Larsen nodded, so did Rodriguez. They walked back to their cruiser. Victor watched them carefully. Fat cops, pizza stains on their uniforms. Overweight and unkempt. He waited for them to drive away. Waited. Waited. He went back inside and closed the door behind him. His mother was snoring in the corner, her oxygen machine hissing. She was fat, too. Had crumbs on her chest. Fat and unkempt. He was waiting for her to die. Waiting. Waiting. Always waiting.

# Daryl

D aryl sat at the kitchen table, fumbling with a pocket knife and scraping dirt from underneath his short fingernails. Melissa would be back from her walk soon. She'd been taking a walk every evening lately. Daryl didn't know why, but he figured she was on some diet kick. Happened every once in a while. He was going tell her about the boat, see what her reaction was. Hopefully she wouldn't get angry, give him a bunch of crap about how they couldn't afford it. Either way, he was going this Saturday to look at boats.

Melissa walked in, holding some light weights in her hands. She glanced at Daryl but didn't say anything. She sat the weights down on the floor then walked over to the sink and poured a glass of water. Still didn't say anything to him. He let her stand there, facing the window, and drink her water.

Finally Daryl spoke. "I'm going up to Dallas this Saturday to look at boats."

Melissa didn't say anything. But she breathed deeply, like she was steeling herself for a fight. Let her. He'd been ready for this. Wanting it. Tired of being told no, especially when he worked so hard.

"Daryl, we've talked about this," she said. "Can't you wait?"

"No."

She finally turned and looked at him. "Can't we compromise on this? Just put it off for another six months?"

"My whole life has been a compromise."

She didn't have anything to say to that. Melissa glared at him for a few seconds. He acted like he didn't see it, just kept picking at his nails with the knife. She gulped down some more water. Daryl watched her, saw the sweat on her forehead glisten. She was still a pretty woman. Not for her age. Just plain pretty. But she wouldn't stop nagging him, holding him back.

"I trust you, Daryl," she said. "I do. I know you'll make the right decision. What'll make you happy and what's good for our family."

Daryl didn't acknowledge her. Just kept on picking with his knife. He felt her watching him, but he didn't look up. She didn't sound like she was being sarcastic or baiting him, but he wasn't going to take a chance. Come hell or high water, he was going to Dallas to look at boats.

"I'm just looking on Saturday," he said. "Didn't say I was actually gonna buy a boat."

"Okay." Melissa set the glass of water down and wiped her face with a towel. "I'm making chicken fried steak for supper. With gravy."

"Sounds good."

They didn't talk again until supper, and with Dustin around, the conversation was polite, even friendly. But they didn't talk about boats or Dallas or compromise at all, even when they sank into bed at around ten o'clock. They laid on their sides and faced away from each other as they fell asleep.

Daryl stared into the dark and thought about Trisha. He

pictured himself lounging with her on the deck of a boat, both of them with drinks in hand. The sun would be warm on their skin and they would drift around whatever lake they chose. They would forget about everything else on land and just enjoy each other. He couldn't imagine anything better.

# Melissa

Daryl wasn't going to come home for supper. Melissa knew that. But she still made the supper she'd planned, homemade enchiladas. She set a plate for him, like she'd been doing, and put on a positive face for Dustin. But neither of them said much, and they both stared at the empty chair where Daryl should have been sitting.

Melissa didn't eat much. She was determined to lose weight. She'd already lost five pounds. She planned to lose fifteen more. Dustin finished his food and went to his room. Melissa cleaned the kitchen and then went and sat on the porch. She brought the cordless phone and a cup of coffee. She sat there and listened to the crickets crying out, singing to their mates. She wondered if any of them had been abandoned.

She dialed Sherry Branch's number and waited. Melissa wasn't really in the mood to talk to the perky pastor's wife. But she needed to hear someone tell her things were going to be okay. The phone rang three times before Sherry picked up.

"Hello?"

"Hey, Sherry, it's Melissa."

"Hey girl! Everything okay?"

"Yeah, I think so," Melissa said. "I just...I guess I just need some encouragement."

"I understand. We all need that sometimes. How are things with you and Daryl?"

Melissa rubbed the arm of the chair. "About the same. He told me he's going to look at boats on Saturday."

"And what'd you say?"

"I didn't try and stop him," Melissa said. "Just like you said. Didn't want to be a nag. I told him I trusted him."

"Well, it sounds like you did the right thing. Just support him, make sure you submit to his decisions. I know that sounds crazy right now, but God made him leader of your house. If you just keep giving him good advice, he'll make the right decision."

"I hope so."

"Girl, just trust God. Get rid of that doubt. There's times we can't see what he's doing, but that's why it's called faith, right?"

Melissa closed her eyes and sighed. "Right."

"Well, I've got to go, hon, but I'll see you Sunday, right?"

"Yes, we'll be there."

"Alright, I'll be praying for y'all. Bye."

"Bye."

Melissa hung up the phone and set it in her lap. The wind picked up and blew warm air all around her. It felt good. She wanted to smile, but couldn't. She wondered where Daryl was and if he was making good decisions. Decisions that would help their family.

# Dustin

The day was beginning to die, the last gasps of sunlight fading through the trees. Dustin noticed the woods taking on a dark, hazy tone and decided not to risk a chance encounter with an angry wild hog. He found the old cow trail that led out of the woods and started walking as fast as he could.

The trail ended near Lane's trailer. He glanced over and saw Lane sitting on the tiny porch that had been built onto the back. Dustin waved, and Lane waved back. That seemed like an invitation, so Dustin walked over, trying hard not to run. But it was hard, because he was excited. When he got close to the porch, he detected the lingering smell of smoke. Lane sat in a dirty plastic chair which might have been white at some point but was now dingy. A bottle of some sort of liquor sat at his feet.

"Any luck?" Lane asked.

Dustin shook his head. Lane nodded to the empty chair beside him, so Dustin climbed the three steps and sat down. The chair looked dirty, but Dustin didn't want to act like a little dirt would bother him.

"If you don't mind my asking, exactly what do you plan to do if you find this panther you're looking for?" Lane asked.

"I don't know."

"Might wanna figure that out before you track him down."

"Yeah."

"So what do you do when you're not tracking down large predators?"

"I don't know," Dustin said. "Usual stuff. I play baseball."

"Oh yeah? What position do you play?"

"Third base. Outfield sometimes."

"I used to pitch," Lane said. "Up until high school. Batters kept getting better. I didn't."

They were quiet for a little while, listening to a whippoorwill call out from the woods. Dustin usually felt awkward when there was silence around adults, but with Lane it felt okay. He didn't feel the need the fill the silence. Neither did Lane, it seemed. Dustin just leaned back in his chair and stared at the sky, which was purple tinged with streaks of orange.

"Shouldn't you be getting home?" Lane asked.

"I don't really wanna go."

"Why not?"

Dustin hesitated. "My parents fight a lot."

"Parents are apt to do that."

"I don't like to be in the house when they do," Dustin said.

Lane picked up the bottle of liquor and took a quick drink. "Don't blame you."

Dustin listened to the woods, hoping to hear the panther make some noise. Some sort of proof that he was real and not some fantasy Dustin had conjured up in his mind. And then he wondered if he *had* imagined the panther and was looking for attention. But he knew what he'd seen. He knew it.

"I saw you at church on Sunday," Dustin said. "And on Wednesday night."

"Yup."

"I don't like church much. Too boring."

"Likewise."

"Then why'd you go?"

"Why'd you go?" Lane asked.

"My parents make me. You're a grownup. You don't have to go."

Lane took another drink. "I don't know. Sometimes you do things 'cause your gut tells you to."

"Your gut?"

"Yeah, like your instincts."

"Your gut." Dustin thought a moment. "What about Miss Wendy?"

"What?"

"Miss Wendy. I saw you talking to her at church."

"You don't miss much, do you?"

"Nope."

Lane smiled. "I will admit that Miss Wendy is the reason I came back on Wednesday. I enjoy talking to her."

"She's pretty."

"She is."

And then they stopped talking for a little while, the whippoorwill the only sound coming from the woods. Mosquitoes were scarce, and Dustin thought that was odd. He had a lot of questions he wanted to ask Lane but didn't want to bug him.

"Your mom gonna worry about you?" Lane asked.

"Not for a little bit."

"Okay."

The stars were just beginning to emerge, barely visible against the purple night sky that hung above the pine trees. Dustin liked how they slowly snuck out from the darkness to shine.

"Why don't you have a job?" Dustin asked.

Lane looked at him for a few seconds before answering. "You got lots of questions."

Dustin shrugged. "I got questions."

"I worked before I moved here," Lane said. "I saved my money, so now I can work a little less."

"Oh."

Lane took another drink, this one really long, until the bottle was empty. He set the bottle down hard and it fell over. Dustin watched it roll to the edge of the porch, but it didn't go over. Lane watched the woods with cloudy eyes, and Dustin thought maybe he saw something. Maybe the panther. But he didn't say anything. Lane just kept staring, looking at something Dustin couldn't see and then Dustin thought that maybe the thing he couldn't see was in the past.

"You should get on home," Lane said. "Before your mama worries."

"Okay."

Dustin climbed down the stairs, looked out toward the woods one more time, and then started walking away from the porch. Lane was still looking out into the woods, into the past.

"Dustin?"

Dustin stopped and looked up at Lane, sitting there on the rickety porch.

"You can stop by and talk anytime you want, alright?"

Dustin nodded.

"Like when your parents are fighting," Lane said. "Or just to talk."

"Okay."

"And keep me updated on the panther hunt, you hear?"

"I will."

Lane nodded at him. Dustin waved and started walking home. When he was a little ways off from the trailer, he looked back over his shoulder. Lane was still staring off in to the woods, staring off into the past.

# Lane

Fog hung over the field behind Lane's trailer, creeping tendrils extending into the woods. He stood on his porch, staring into the trees, half expecting to see Dustin's panther. But there was nothing there, only darkness. He got in his truck and drove over to Wendy's house. He wasn't real comfortable going over there, just being friendly with a woman again, but she was drawing him to her somehow.

Wendy's place wasn't too hard to find. Only a few miles away, right off the farm-to-market road that led to Crow Valley. A white wooden house sat about fifty yards off the blacktop. The paint was flaking off a bit. There were a few flowers growing in front of the house, but otherwise not much landscaping. Lane pulled up next to Wendy's car, then walked to the front door and knocked on the screen door.

Wendy appeared after a few seconds. She stood behind the screen door, looking up at him, like she was surprised to see him.

Lane just stared back, looked into her eyes. He liked how she wasn't too shy, wasn't afraid to look him in the eye. A lot of girls were either bashful or faked it. He didn't care for either.

Wendy pushed open the door. "Hey."

"Morning."

"Have any trouble finding the place?"

Lane shook his head.

"Have you had breakfast?"

Lane hadn't slept or ate. Those dreams, they kept him up all night. And the alcohol wasn't working anymore. He hadn't eaten because the sour taste of liquor was left over in his mouth.

"Thanks, but I already ate."

"Okay."

Wendy crossed her arms and looked over at her car. Lane thought she might be nervous. Maybe she was. He wasn't good at picking up body language.

"Let's have a look at your car," Lane said.

They walked over to it. Wendy popped the hood, and Lane began poking around inside for a few minutes. He asked a few questions, check some fluids, then shut the hood. The car wasn't in too bad shape. It just needed some work.

"I'm gonna head to town real quick, pick up some things I need," Lane said. "Shouldn't take long."

"Okay."

Lane drove to town and found an auto parts store. He spent a couple hundred bucks on what he needed, ordered a few other parts, then headed back. On the way back, he heard a song on the radio, an old country song, and it made him kind of sad. Almost nostalgic.

When he got back to Wendy's, he pulled his truck around closer to her car and got out all his tools and the parts he'd just bought. Wendy came out on the porch, arms crossed, staring out at him. He waved at her, and she waved back. The fog had burned off by then, and the air was becoming muggy.

Lane started by changing the battery and the battery cables. After that, he changed the oil, something easy. Usually he'd tackle the hard tasks first, but he wanted to get as much done as possible today. When he was pouring new oil into the engine, Wendy came out of the house with a large glass of water. She handed it to him, and he started gulping.

"I feel bad, you being out here working and me ignoring you," she said. "Like you're some stranger I hired to work on my car."

"Kinda how it is. Except the hiring part."

"You know what I mean."

"You wanna help?" Lane asked.

"I don't think I'd be much help."

"You could sit and keep me company," Lane said.

"I can do that."

Wendy got a large towel out of the trunk of the car and spread it on the ground. She crossed her legs and sat down while Lane started changing some hoses which were one hot day from cracking in two. He felt Wendy's eyes on him while he loosened the clamps on a hose.

"You could talk some," Lane said. "You know, make it less awkward."

"You don't strike me as a person that minds awkwardness."

Lane removed the old hose. "Well, we could get to know each other. Ask questions, stuff like that."

"You just want me to volunteer all my personal information? Without a proper dinner?"

"I suppose that was silly of me."

The day was already heating up, sweat was forming on Lane's forehead. He looked over at Wendy and saw her face glistening, too. The humidity could press down on you, like you were wearing another layer of skin. But it was better than Houston, which was a swamp with tall buildings.

"I'll answer one question," Wendy said. "Only one."

Lane started putting the clamps on the new hose. "Guess I better make it a good one."

Wendy smiled and nodded. Lane thought for a moment, considered his options. A crow landed on the ground about twenty yards away from them and cawed a few times. They both watched him peck around the ground.

"If you could take any vacation, what would it be?" Lane asked.

"Money's not a problem?"

Lane shook his head.

"Easy," Wendy said. "Some island in the Caribbean, don't care which one. Just me and a stack of books by the beach."

"You like to read, huh?"

"Yes. Right up there on that porch, up until July or August, when it gets too hot. Then I move inside and sit on a recliner in front of the AC we have in the window."

Lane loosened a pulley and then yanked out a drive belt that was almost ripped to shreds. He looked at it for a minute and then threw it on the ground, shaking his head.

"Do you like to read?" Wendy asked.

Lane shook his head. "Not really. There's been a few I've liked, though."

"I love reading. Read a book a week, maybe every two weeks."

"What book you reading right now?" Lane asked.

Wendy's face lit up. "I'll show you."

She jumped up and ran into the house, the screen door banging shut behind her. Her enthusiasm made Lane feel good, gave him energy. Made him remember how it felt to want to do something, be a man, not just surviving but attacking the day like a warrior. Wendy came back with three books in her hand. She sat down and put the stack in front of her.

"So I'm reading three books right now," she said.

"Okay."

She held up a ratty paperback with a dark cover. "This one is by John Grisham. I love his stuff, makes me feel like a lawyer. Like I could actually understand all that legal stuff."

Lane just smiled and grunted as he put in the new belt, weaving it through the pulleys. Wendy set down the Grisham book.

"This one's *Blue Like Jazz*." Wendy held up a purple book for Lane to see.

"So you like jazz music?"

"No, it's not like that. The jazz is a metaphor for faith, or something like that."

"Oh," Lane said. "I think I get it."

"It's a good book. You should read it."

Lane tightened the tension pulley. "I might if you let me borrow it."

"When I finish it."

Wendy picked up the third book. "This one is really good, but I don't think you'd like it. It's kind of self-help stuff, but with a Christian message."

"Okay."

"It's by a pastor up in Dallas," Wendy said. "David Waters. Ever heard of him?"

"Can't say that I have."

"He's the pastor of Life Rising Church. It's a pretty big church up there. Anyway, this book is called *Expecting to Rise*. It's about expecting good things to come to you because God loves you."

Lane put a jack under the car and started lifting it up. "You're right. I don't think I'd care for that one. Probably stick with the Grisham if it was up to me."

"I don't know, it's got some good stuff in it. I haven't finished it, but what I have read gets me pumped up. I mean, I know it's kind of hokey and stuff, but it makes me feel like every day can be great, can be an adventure. Every day can be a blessing."

"Not every day," Lane said from beneath the car.

He felt bad saying it, but he didn't care for books that were all sunshine and rainbows. Life wasn't like that. Lots of rain clouds blocking the sunlight. But he wasn't going to tell her that, this woman who believed that things could be better. Believed that he could be better. And she had to, otherwise she wouldn't be sitting here talking to him. Wendy was smart, intuitive. She'd probably already smelled the liquor on his breath, seen his bloodshot eyes. But she was still

77

sitting here talking to him.

"You want me to read some to you?" Wendy asked.

"Not that book," Lane replied. "The purple one."

"*Blue Like Jazz*?"

"Yeah. I like metaphors."

Wendy started reading and Lane removed the starter from the car. He liked the writing in the book, but more than that, he liked the sound of Wendy's voice. It was smooth and melodic and precise. He wanted her to read this book to him and then another and then the story of her life until her voice was hoarse and she could read no more.

# Victor

Victor sat in his backyard, in one of those folding lawn chairs that was never too comfortable. Beside him, on a rickety card table, sat a tall glass of lemonade and a jar of crickets. He watched the sunset over the thin conglomeration of oaks and pines that bordered his property. The pink-orange sky soothed him, made him feel calm.

He needed it. An electricity surged in him, from his heart all the way out to the tips of his fingers. The money was already being spent in his mind. But not in a material way, because Victor was too intelligent for that. Yes, yes he was. That money didn't mean having lots of things. No, if getting things was all he wanted, there were easier ways to go about it. That money meant freedom. Blessed freedom, like in the hymns he'd grown up singing.

But he had to wait. Wait and wait and wait. The police had the old man on their radar now. Which didn't mean anything.

Except that Victor had to be patient. Waiting, waiting, always waiting. Slow and steady wins the race. Yes, he had to be patient. He'd always mowed the old man's yard every other Tuesday. So he couldn't go over there until then. And then when he was there, he could find what he was looking for, what he needed for freedom. It would even make him look good, keeping up the old man's property for no pay. Generous, self-sacrificing. All those terms the sheep he lived among used. Had to wait just a while longer.

Victor took a cricket out of the jar and let it squirm in his hand. He smiled a little, passing it from hand to hand. Then he ripped its legs off and wondered if crickets screamed like they sang. He bit its head off and felt the juices flow through his mouth and down his throat. Patience, sweet patience.

# Daryl

Through no intention of his own, Daryl ended up outside of Shelley's talking with Trisha. She just happened to be leaving about the same time as he was finishing up his burger. So he walked her out, and now they were leaning up against his pickup, talking. He kept smelling her perfume over the grease of the diner, and every time he did he felt a heat rise up in his body, like when he was a teenager.

Trisha was telling him about some customer who threw a fit earlier in her shift, but Daryl wasn't listening. His eyes moved over her hair, her eyes, her lips, all of her. He kept looking at her skin, how soft it looked, and he had to stop himself from reaching out to run his fingers over it. To feel skin on skin, that's what he wanted.

"Anyway, what you been doing?" Trisha asked.

"Oh, just working," Daryl said. "You know how it is."

"Yeah."

"Went looking at boats last weekend, though."

Daryl said this to her just because it was what he'd done over the weekend. It was only after the words left his mouth that he realized buying a boat might impress this girl. And it was only when he thought of her as a girl did he wonder about her age and begin thinking of a graceful way to ask her how many birthdays she'd celebrated.

"That's cool," Trisha said. "What kinda boats?"

"Big ones. Like a pontoon boat."

"Really? I thought you'd say something like a bass boat or even a canoe."

Daryl smiled slightly. "No, I want something big. Been saving up for a long time."

"That's cool, man. I love boats."

When she said this Daryl felt good, real good. About himself and her and everything in between. He wanted to get a little closer, feel their bodies touch.

"I got pictures of the ones I'm looking at," Daryl said.

"Lemme see."

Daryl pulled out his cell phone and flipped it open. After he pushed a few buttons, he found the pictures of the boats he'd looked at Dallas.

"You can't see them too good," Daryl said. "My camera doesn't take good pictures."

"Least you got a phone."

Daryl laughed. Trisha took the phone from him and started looking at the pictures. He moved a little closer and looked over her shoulder. He could smell her perfume better, feel the heat of her body perfectly. Kissing her would have been easy, right there and then, and something told him she wouldn't have had a problem with it. But it was a line, a clear line he could see easily, that he wasn't ready to cross. If someone had asked him why he wasn't ready to jump over it and forget it completely, he wouldn't have been able to explain it.

"Man, I love going out on boats," Trisha said. "Love just floating in the water, sitting in the sun. When you finally get one, you're gonna have to take me out."

Daryl's heart raced a little. He wanted to take this girl somewhere right now and lay with her and be as close as God intended man and woman to be. But all his life he'd been something, been a certain kind of man. He knew if he touched this girl he'd be something different. Something unlike himself. Standing next to Trisha, though, was like drinking strong whiskey and every moment was like another shot, burning his throat. It was easy to lose control.

"I've already got a boat," Daryl said. "It's just small. Only enough room for two or three people."

"Shoot, I'm a country girl. That's good enough for me. More boat than I've got."

"Yeah."

"So you'll take me out on it?" Trisha brushed a golden lock away from her forehead, blinked her eyes. "I ain't been on a boat in a long time. Small or big."

Daryl hesitated, but only for a second. "Yeah. What day are you free?"

"I got nothing happening on Tuesday."

"How about meeting me in Stonewall at noon?" Daryl asked. "I know a good place there."

Trisha batted those eye lashes again. "Where at?"

"That gas station on 75 and Harker Road."

"I'll be there."

"Alright, I'd better get on," Daryl said.

"Me too."

Trisha walked about halfway to her car, then turned around and waved at Daryl. He gave her a little nod, then climbed up in his pickup. As he was driving home, he told himself he wasn't going to do anything but give the girl a ride in his boat. But he felt that heat rise in him, his blood pumping strong throughout his body. And he thought about Melissa, who was probably at home in bed.

Daryl just wanted to have a good day, without worrying about life. He couldn't do that with Melissa anymore. Maybe with Trisha he could.

# Melissa

nother night setting a plate for a man who wouldn't be there to eat. Melissa was beginning to think she was some sort of crazy. After dinner, she'd started making cookies. She told herself it was for Dustin, so the boy could have a treat. She even put in extra chocolate chips for him. But really, it was to keep her hands busy. She needed to keep moving. She'd cleaned more in the past couple of weeks than the rest of the year. If she kept busy, she was able to forget that her husband was never home and seemed happy to ignore his family.

She'd been able to lose weight. Not a lot, but it was slowly starting to come off. Little by little, her pants and dresses were getting looser in the waist. It made her happy, and she felt better, but it didn't seem to be having any effect on Daryl. They barely spoke to each other. He never touched her. None of those loving shoulder rubs, or kisses on the cheek. Nothing.

She pulled the cookies out of the oven and brought a few to

Dustin with a large glass of milk. He was in his room, and she didn't usually let him take food there, but a lot of things didn't seem to matter lately. So she let him eat cookies on the floor of his bedroom while he read about panthers in a book he'd gotten from the library. He'd been obsessed with panthers lately, even said he saw one in the woods. She believed him, because Dustin was honest, always had been, but Daryl had told her it was impossible, and she trusted him, too.

"Thanks, Mama," Dustin said.

"You're welcome, sweetie."

"Do you know when Dad's getting home?"

"No," Melissa said, shaking her head. "I'm not sure."

"Okay."

Her little boy said it was okay, but she knew it wasn't. Dustin had been following Daryl around like a puppy all his life, and now his daddy was gone, and he couldn't understand why. And for the hundredth time Melissa wondered what she'd done wrong, because she was certain Dustin was innocent. She knew Daryl stilled loved him unconditionally. He was just distracted by something, so he was forgetting his little boy. And she knew Daryl was human, was just a man, and people forgot things, even important things sometimes. How many houses had burned down because someone forgot about a burner on the stove being on?

"I'm gonna go read a little on the porch, okay?" Melissa bent down and kissed Dustin's forehead.

"Okay."

On the way out she grabbed a handful of cookies and ate them all quickly. She knew it would set her back, make her gain some weight, but she needed some sort of pleasure. Something good. Even if that good was only a short burst of pleasure from sugar and empty calories. She settled on a chair on the porch and tried to read the book Sherry had recommended. The author used women from the Bible as examples of how to be a godly wife. But all it made her think was that if Daryl could, he'd just add another wife to his house, and Melissa would probably have to sleep in another bedroom by herself.

So instead of reading she just cried quietly. No sobs, no heart-wrenching cries to God. Just tears flowing down her face like a fountain. She cried until there were no tears left. And then she waited to go inside so Dustin wouldn't worry about her crying. She didn't want to upset the boy.

She cleaned up the kitchen and said goodnight to Dustin, who was so engrossed in his research he barely mumbled anything back. She changed into her nightgown, the one with the floral pattern that she liked so much. It was soft. She didn't bother looking in the mirror at her figure. So many calories in those cookies.

Melissa turned off all the lights and lay in bed, staring up at the ceiling. She'd been having trouble falling asleep until Daryl came home. When his side of the bed was empty, she wondered where he was, what he'd been doing. She'd started looking for signs of an affair. But Daryl didn't smell like any kind of perfume, didn't take showers when he got home, and she'd found no notes or unusual expenses in their bank account. Which honestly might be worse, she thought to herself. At least if he was sleeping with someone else he'd have a reason to be away from us. But he just didn't want to be at home, didn't want to be with his family.

She laid there in the dark for a long time. How long she didn't know, because she didn't dare look at the clock. A watched pot never boils and all that. Melissa didn't want to know how long she waited for her husband to come to their bed.

Daryl finally did come home. Melissa turned away from his side of the bed, trying to pretend like she was sleeping. Daryl didn't turn his lamp on though, like he usually did. She heard him undressing in the dark, and she thought it was weird, but whatever. Who knew what was going on anymore?

He climbed into bed and was suddenly near her. In that moment they touched more than in the last week combined. Daryl pulled her toward him and was pulling her nightgown off before she even realized what was happening. She lifted her arms so it would be easier, and he tossed the gown on the floor. Her eyes had adjusted to the dark but she could still barely see him. Mostly just his figure.

And then they were kissing, deeply and sloppily, like teenagers. Melissa was confused but then decided to shut her mind down and let her husband sweep her away to wherever he wanted to take her. He did, too. His hands were all over her, everywhere. They tossed and turned for some time, and when they were through, Melissa didn't bother dressing, just in case Daryl decided to take her up again. Which he did, about an hour later.

Melissa didn't sleep all night, whether from the physical activity or the excitement of Daryl coming home to her or both. She just laid there in bed, staring at the ceiling, sweaty and smiling.

# Wendy

verything had been perfect. Absolutely perfect. A better date couldn't be found in a movie. She'd felt this way before and knew it might not last. She was older now, more mature and definitely more experienced. A guy couldn't slip some bull crap past her. Not anymore. She'd earned her stripes, as they say. Just thinking that made her laugh.

Lane had picked her up on time, which mattered, and they'd gone to the Mexican restaurant in Crow Valley. Over tortilla chips and salsa they'd made some awkward conversation, and then the small talk continued while they ate enchiladas and tacos. But it was what she wanted. They were practically strangers, just getting to know each other.

After they finished the food, Lane asked if she wanted to the next town over, Union City, to see a movie or go bowling. But that didn't seem right for them, to do something everybody does on a date. Maybe some other time. Wendy didn't want to be distracted by a movie or the loud clatter of falling bowling pins. She wanted Lane all to herself.

So she suggested that they drive all over Crow County. Lane looked confused, then amused, and finally agreeable. Wendy took him riding all over the back roads, pointing out the houses of people she knew and telling stories about riding these dirt roads herself as a teenager. They rolled the windows down and turned the radio up. She sang along to George Strait, Reba McEntire, and Garth Brooks. Lane just drove and smiled at her.

Now they were on her porch, sitting in a swing, rocking back and forth. Wendy wanted to reach out and grab Lane's hand. It was right beside her. But she thought it'd be too aggressive, and she'd already been pretty forthright. It was time for Lane to make some moves. Not that he seemed bashful. More like wary.

"This was good," Wendy said. "I had fun."

"Me too."

"So can I ask a question?"

"Just one?"

"Well, we'll start with one," Wendy replied. "But I'll go as long as you let me. I'm a curious girl."

"Curiosity killed the cat."

"Yeah, well, this cat ain't dead yet."

"Fire away."

"How'd you end up here?" Wendy asked. "You know, since your parents are gone, and you're not really from here."

"Well, it just sort of worked out this way. They're out seeing the world, running around in an RV somewhere."

"Really? Where?"

"I don't know. Last time I spoke with them they were in Virginia, headed south from there."

"And so you're here because..."

Lane turned his head slightly toward her and took a deep breath. "Guess I just needed some peace and quiet. Get away from the city, all that traffic and noise."

"Which city?"

"Houston."

"Oh." Wendy fought the urge to lay her head on his shoulder. "What'd you do there?"

"Thought it was just one question."

Wendy shrugged.

"I was a mechanic," Lane said.

Wendy smiled. "Now it all makes sense."

"You've solved the mystery."

"So you quit and moved here?"

"Yes."

"Living rent free with your parents," Wendy said. "I know the feeling."

Lane smiled. "What about you?"

"What?"

"What're you doing here?"

"In Crow Valley?"

"Crow Valley, your grandma's house, the dentist's office," Lane said. "All of it."

Wendy looked at the ground. "That's a lot, and it's getting late."

"Give me the short version."

"Well, it's a pretty average story," Wendy said. "Lived here my whole life, went to college, got married, got divorced, moved back here. And now I'm on a porch swing with you."

"So you were married?" Lane asked.

"Yes. That change anything?"

"Nope." Lane hesitated for a few moments. "How long ago did it end?"

"About five years ago."

"I see."

"What about you?" Wendy asked.

"Yeah. It ended little more than a year ago."

"So we're in the same boat."

"Close enough," Lane said.

They rocked back and forth for a long time, listening to the rusty chains on the swing creak. Crickets sang to them as a humid dew started falling on the ground. Wendy loved this time of summer, before the heat became dry and fierce. She could feel Lane fidgeting beside her and knew he was uncomfortable talking about all this. But she pressed on.

"Is that the reason you drink?" Wendy asked.

Lane only looked at her.

"I smell it on you. You try to hide it but you can't."

He nodded. "I drink too much."

"Yeah."

"Is it a problem for you?"

Wendy took his hand. "I'm still here, aren't I?"

Lane sighed, deep and heavy. She squeezed his hand tight, and they rocked back and forth under the stars. They stayed that way for hours.

Close to midnight, Granny came out and sat down with them. Her hip gave her trouble sometimes and she wasn't able to sleep. At first, Wendy was concerned Lane would feel like Granny was intruding on their date. But she saw his face when Granny sat down in the rocking chair across from them. He smiled widely and apologized for making too much noise. It was then that Wendy felt the first sharp pangs of what she knew to be love.

The three of them talked for another hour, and Lane never let go of her hand.

# Daryl

The Outpost was a junky little gas station in the middle of nowhere that was poorly maintained. It didn't have to be nice, though, because it sat at a cross roads near a lake and a state park and was the only gas station within miles. They sold bait and tackle, too, as well as some pretty good barbecue sandwiches. With all the traffic coming and going, Daryl figured he wouldn't draw too much attention.

When he pulled into the parking lot, Trisha was already waiting, leaning up against her car. She was wearing blue jean shorts and a white t-shirt. Simple, but she made it look good. He pulled up behind her and left the truck running as he got out. Typically people with boats parked in a large gravel area to the east of the gas station, but he wanted to grab Trisha and get going. Daryl didn't think he'd see anyone he knew there, but he couldn't be sure.

"Hey there," Daryl said.

"Hey." Trisha walked over to the boat and put a hand on it.

"Pretty nice."

"Just a little fishing boat. The one I want is a lot bigger."

"Well, it's better than my boat."

Daryl laughed. "You ready?"

"Yeah."

Daryl nodded toward the truck. Trisha grabbed a small bag from her car and then climbed into the cab with him. Once the doors were closed he could smell her, a mixture of perfume and sun tan lotion. It made his adrenaline pump, and his head swim. He remembered the tightness in his chest from a couple weeks ago and thought how this felt exactly the opposite. They cruised down the highway with the radio humming in the background, some old country song he'd heard since he was a child.

"So we're going to the lake?" Trisha asked.

"No, we're going to a friend's place. I helped him out a few years ago with some people poaching on his land, so he said I could fish on his lake anytime I wanted. We're gonna go over there. It's not too far from here."

"Our own private lake, huh?"

"Sort of."

They drove a little farther down the road, then turned onto a little dirt road that was barely big enough for the truck. After about a hundred yards, they came to a gate. Daryl put the truck in park and got out. There was a combination lock on the gate, and after he put in the numbers, he glanced over at Trisha. He wondered if she was as nervous as he was.

They crawled along the tiny road until they came to the lake, which was actually just a very large pond. But it was big enough to get a boat into and tool around for a little bit. Usually he came here to fish, but he didn't bring any poles today. He wasn't sure what they were going to do out there on the lake. Probably talk. Most women liked that.

There wasn't a boat ramp at this private lake. But he'd been here several times, so he knew where there was a good spot to put in. It didn't take long to get the boat into the water. Trisha grabbed her

93

bag, and Daryl grabbed a cooler with bottled water and a couple sandwiches. In a few minutes they were speeding around the lake, the engine screaming behind them. He showed her around, took her through all the nooks and crannies. After about an hour, he went to the middle of the lake and turned off the engine. He didn't bother dropping anchor. They were happy to float.

Daryl opened the cooler and handed Trisha a bottle of water. She took it and sipped it. He leaned back in his seat, looked up at the sky. It was so blue and wide. He put his hand in the lake, felt the cool water on his hand. God, he loved this. All of it.

"This is nice," Trisha said. "Just floating like this. So peaceful."

"Yeah, I try to do this as much as I can. Helps me relax."

"I'll bet."

Trisha set the water down at her feet and then lifted her shirt over her head. She set the shirt beside her and grabbed a bottle of sun tan lotion out of her bag. Daryl let his eyes linger on her. She was wearing a red bikini top, and the shorts hung low on her hips. She was thin, but not unhealthy. He could see her ribs, all the way up to the fabric of the top. Trisha noticed him looking at her.

"It's more than halfway through June, and I'm still pale as a ghost," she said. "I've been working so much I haven't been able to get some sun."

Daryl nodded slowly, as if he were thinking about her tan. She handed the bottle to him.

"Put some on my back."

He took the bottle and just stared at it. Trisha turned to the side so he could reach her back. He squirted a little bit of the lotion into his hand and then began rubbing it into her back. Her soft skin sent jolts of electricity up his arms and into his lungs. He lost his breath. Daryl memorized the freckles on her back, the smooth curves of her hips and the slender muscles in her shoulders. After the lotion disappeared into her skin, he leaned back into his seat.

Trisha pulled sunglasses out of the bag and looked up at the sky. Daryl wondered if she was thinking about it like he had, how blue and wide it was and always over them. His breaths were shallow, almost like a panic.

"I'm married," he said. Just blurted it out.

Trisha slowly lowered her head until she was looking at him. "I figured."

"I mean, we're not getting along real well, though."

"I figured that, too." She dipped her hand into the water, splashed it a bit. "I've got a boyfriend."

Daryl nodded.

"I mean a serious one," she said. "We've been living together for a couple years."

"Alright."

"My mama hates it. Us being shacked up without being married."

"I guess y'all are having problems, too," Daryl said.

"The honeymoon is definitely over."

"Does he know you're here?"

"Your wife know you're here?" Trisha asked.

Daryl didn't answer. Trisha smiled, but she wasn't mocking him or being smart. Just stating the obvious. They sat in silence for a while, calmed by the gentle rocking of the boat. They drifted over to a dead tree sticking up out of the water. It was skinny and white, and to Daryl it looked like a bone.

"Let's just enjoy this," Trisha said. "Not think about anything but what a nice day this is."

"Sounds alright to me."

"You said you had sandwiches, right?"

They floated for a while, eating sandwiches and drinking water, making small talk. Daryl carefully avoided mentioning Melissa and Trisha did the same. Mostly they sat in silence, listening to the birds and watching fish jump out of the water. After a little while, Trisha laid down near the bow of the boat, stretching out as much as she could. Daryl stared at her body. His hands ached to touch her skin again.

Around four o'clock Daryl guided the boat back to shore, and with Trisha's help dragged it back up onto the trailer. They drove back to the gas station, the radio playing in the background. They weren't talking a lot, but somehow it was okay, wasn't awkward. Daryl parked behind her car again. Trisha got out and walked around to his window.

"Thanks for taking me out there," she said. "It was fun."

"Anytime."

"Don't say that." She tucked a few strands of hair behind her ear. "I'll make you bring me out there all the time."

"Wouldn't be the worst thing in the world."

Trisha smiled and pushed his shoulder. Daryl smiled and his heart jumped at the contact between them.

"Let me see your phone."

Daryl handed the phone out the window, then watched her push buttons for a few moments. She handed the phone back to him.

"My number's in there now. Give me a call whenever."

"Alright."

Trisha waved to him, then got in her car. He pulled out of the gas station and got on the road back toward Crow Valley. His head was buzzing, and he couldn't get the image of Trisha sun bathing out of his mind.

# Melissa

Melissa was no longer walking. She was jogging, dropping pounds like crazy. Some of her pants didn't fit at all anymore. She had to go and buy new clothes, which was okay with her. As long as it was a smaller size. She'd also stopped with the junk food, and found she had more energy.

And then there was Daryl. He'd been more affectionate, more caring lately. He was even holding her in bed, tightly. A lot of times it was hot but she didn't care. It was like when they first married, all those years ago. It was like her husband had come back to life. At least during the night.

Now they were here at this steak restaurant, and it was his idea. They'd dropped Dustin off at a friend's house for the evening, which was something the boy needed. He was completely focused on finding that panther, the one Daryl kept assuring her didn't exist. Dustin needed some time to just have fun.

For the most part, Melissa didn't talk too much. She was

worried she'd say something that might ruin this transformation. So she asked questions about work and listened to Daryl's stories with delight. She didn't care if it was boring or not. She was just glad her husband was happy to be with her again.

He talked about buying a boat while Melissa savored the steak and potatoes on her plate. She suppressed a smile when he mentioned a smaller one might be better after all. The only thing that worried her is that Daryl wanted to get one as soon as possible. They could work it out later.

It looked like Sherry knew what she was talking about. Those books, too. Maybe she and Daryl had let themselves get into a rut. She was partly to blame. They'd gotten comfortable, stopped caring about their relationship. Now that she'd put in the effort, Daryl was paying attention, too. She'd been praying hard, begging and pleading with God to make her husband love her again. Sometimes prayers are answered.

After sharing dessert, a large piece of chocolate pie, they drove home and enjoyed having the house to themselves. Just like when they were first married. Daryl fell asleep in her arms. Melissa stroked his hair, which was starting to thin a little but still looked good and felt soft. He murmured in his sleep, saying things she couldn't understand. She smiled, breathed deep and fell asleep too.

# Dustin

Standing on the creek bank, Dustin peered into the large hole on the opposite bank. It was dark and tree roots lined its edges, like skeleton fingers. He wanted to see what was in it, but he was scared. When he imagined finding the panther, it wasn't like this. Not cornering it in a hole and giving it nowhere to go except through him.

But he had to check it out. So he followed the creek downstream a little ways, until he found an easy place to cross. Then he traveled back upstream until he was standing over the hole. He surveyed the situation, then found the easiest way down into the hole. He decided it was better to not think about it. Otherwise he might lose his courage.

Dustin slid down the bank on dead pine needles about five feet, using small saplings to steady himself. He hit level ground in front of the hole, which was about four feet wide. He squatted down and looked in, but there wasn't much he could see without going right up to the hole and sticking his head in.

So that's what he did.

He wished he had a flashlight, but he was never out here at night. He wasn't stupid. Dustin barely put his head inside the hole, only enough to see. He waited for his eyes to adjust to the darkness, waiting to hear the rumbling growl he sometimes heard in his dreams. His heart pounded as he searched. There were all kind of things to worry about. Snakes, bobcats, maybe scorpions. But he had to see it.

After a little while, the darkness grew discernible, and Dustin saw that the hole wasn't as big as he thought it was. And there was no panther. No anything. He sighed deeply and backed away slowly. But as he did, his hand brushed against something cold. He looked down and saw a bone. It was skinny and white. On the end of it was a hoof, with a little fur around it. A deer leg, he realized. There was dark red blood caked around on the fur and a white stringy piece of flesh hanging. A ligament or tendon. It probably hadn't been dead for very long. Maybe a day or two at most.

Dustin looked around for tracks, his heart pounding harder than before. But there was nothing. He sighed in disappointment, knowing his dad would never believe it was the panther. He'd say it was a bobcat, or a coyote, or even Bigfoot before he admitted it was a panther. He thought about bringing the leg bone back with him, but there was no point. It wouldn't prove anything. Still, he knew the panther had killed a deer and eaten it here.

He looked up at the creek bank and planned a path up. He started up the bank. About halfway up the pine needles and dirt gave way beneath his feet, and he slipped. His instincts kicked in, and he reached out to grab something. He caught onto a pine sapling, but his momentum was already carrying him down. He kept hold of the sapling, though, which made him swing around wildly. As he did, his other arm hit another tree, and a jolt of pain shot through it and up into his chest. He lost his grip and went tumbling.

Dustin rolled down the creek bank and came to rest at the bottom. He laid there for a few seconds, head swimming from the fall. He felt okay, though, except for his left arm, which was screaming in pain. He sat up and looked at his arm. There was a large gash and blood dripping out of it. He wiped his arm with his shirt, which probably wasn't clean and was going to make his mom yell at him, but whatever.

He got up and started to climb the bank again, this time more carefully. At the spot where he slipped he paused and looked. Sure enough, there was a small tree with large thorns sticking out of the branches. He figured he snagged his arm on one of them. He kept moving and got to the top of the bank, where he wiped his arm with his shirt again. It was bad, and that made him upset, almost to tears, because he was going to have to show his mom. She might forbid him from coming down here, or seeing Lane, or ever looking for the panther again. He'd try and clean it up before she saw it.

Dustin found his usual path out of the woods and walked quickly. He wanted to get a bandage on his arm. As he came out of the woods he saw Lane sitting on his porch, smoking a cigarette. Dustin wiped his eyes, just to make sure there weren't any tears. He approached the porch and sat down beside Lane.

"Any luck today?" Lane asked.

Dustin shook his head. His arm was throbbing, but at least the blood had clotted a little. Lane looked over at his arm and raised his eyebrows.

"Got yourself a scratch," he said.

"Yeah."

"How'd that happen?"

"On a tree," Dustin said. "I slipped and then swung my arm out."

"I see." Lane stood up. "Come on inside, and let's clean that up."

Dustin followed Lane into the trailer through a squeaking screen door. They entered into a tiny living room with a small couch and a brown recliner. A couple of steps led them into a small kitchen with a red, wooden table where Lane motioned for Dustin to sit. Lane disappeared down a dark hallway for a few minutes. When he came back, he had a wash cloth, a bottle of hydrogen peroxide, and a large bandage. He grabbed a chair and pulled it up next to Dustin.

"Probably gonna sting," Lane said. He looked into Dustin's eyes. "Can you handle it?"

Dustin was worried, but he nodded confidently. Lane went to the kitchen sink and soaked the wash cloth, then wrung it out. He sat back down and took Dustin's arm in his hands. Dustin's arm felt small in Lane's hands.

"Alright, this is gonna hurt a little," Lane said.

He wiped the wash cloth over Dustin's arm, washing away the dirt and dried blood. He then pressed a little harder, still gentle though, cleaning the wound as best he could. Then he grabbed the bottle of hydrogen peroxide and poured a little on the wash cloth. Lane looked at Dustin for permission, and Dustin nodded. Lane pressed the wash cloth to the wound and held it there firmly. It started stinging badly, and Dustin had to bite his lip to keep from crying out. He didn't want Lane to think he was weak.

"Good job," Lane said. He removed the wash cloth and threw it on the floor. "Let's get a bandage on there."

Lane took the packaging off the bandage and carefully put it on Dustin's arm. It was big but it was flesh colored. Maybe his mom wouldn't notice it. Probably not. She'd been distracted lately, crying and spending a lot of time alone. He didn't like seeing her sad, but she hadn't been all over him lately, so that was good.

"That's a pretty good gash you got there," Lane said. "Probably gonna scar."

"Really?"

"Not bad, but yeah. It'll be alright, though. Chicks dig scars."

"They do?"

"I don't know, man." Lane stood up and threw the packaging in the trash can near the table. "They used to. Times change. There some girl you wanna show off that scar to?"

Dustin's face turned red. "No."

"I'll bet there's one. If not, will be soon enough."

"Maybe one girl," Dustin said. "Becky Roberts."

Lane picked the wash cloth up off the ground and threw it in the sink. "Becky. Nice name."

"Yeah."

"Well, you'll have a story to tell her when you go back to school," Lane said. "Cut your arm open hunting a panther. Good story for a good scar."

Dustin looked down at his arm while Lane rummaged through the fridge. He came over to the table with an orange soda for Dustin and a beer for himself. They sat there in silence for a little while drinking.

"Lane?"

"Yeah."

"Do scars hurt?" Dustin asked. "Even after they've healed?"

Lane took a long drink of his beer. "Yeah, buddy. Sometimes they ache for years and years."

# Lane

The bottle on the small table beside his bed was half empty. Yes, half empty, because Lane had little room for optimism these days. Even taking into consideration the beautiful woman who seemed to enjoy his company, he had no illusions about life and its ability to kick you when you're down.

Lane considered opening the bottle and draining the contents. But he didn't. He was trying to cut back, trying hard. And not just because his body ached from having to filter out the poison he was consuming every day. He wanted to cut back because of Wendy. No matter what she said, nobody wants to be around an alcoholic. They may tolerate them for a time, but that's all.

He was only smoking a few cigarettes every day, but even that felt like too many. He'd never smoked before, not even in high school when it felt cool. Now he couldn't stop. The buzz of the nicotine hitting his system calmed him for a few hours. Made his hands stop shaking.

The cigarettes and booze kept the demons away, kept them out of his mind. A ritual had formed over the past year. Drink, smoke, pray. And Lane had mostly given up on the praying. God didn't answer prayers. At least not his.

He paced the bedroom, glancing over at the bottle from time to time. He reached into his pocket and pulled the ring out of his pocket. It felt heavier than it should. He held it between his middle finger and thumb, but didn't put it on. Never did. He put it in his dresser, next to the other one, sat down on the bed and grabbed the bottle. It felt lighter than it should have.

There was Wendy. Beautiful Wendy who sometimes invaded his dreams and drove the demons away. Lane was coming to understand that he needed her to stay sane, to function and be a man and a human being. She might have some way to snatch him out of the hand of the demons. But she was so high above him, up on a pedestal of some sort, and he couldn't think of any way to get to her. He could keep it together and show up every day, prove that he cared, but he could only do that with the liquor.

Lane took the cap off the bottle and took a long drink because if he didn't he was going to drive over to Wendy's just to see her. Just to talk to her. It was too late for that, and it wasn't something a real man would do. Go whimpering to a woman in the middle of the night like some lost dog. No woman would want that. Wendy wouldn't, and Lane didn't want to be her Christian charity.

No, he wanted to drink until those damn demons were dead, drowned in a sea of burning liquor.

# Wendy

endy came home every day feeling like she was covered in
spit. She hated it, and her day had been especially long. Too
many upset children squirming in the dentist's chair. Not
that she blamed them. She was almost thirty and didn't
care for it herself. But it was late June and the heat was starting to get
to her.

So when she got out of her car and saw Lane doing some
sort of work on the porch she felt irritated. Men. Always trying to
prove how much they can do or how valuable they are. Wendy sighed
as she stomped up the wooden steps. Lane was putting new boards
onto the far end of the porch. He looked up as she reached the top
of the stairs.

"Hey," he said.

"What are you working on now?" Wendy asked.

Lane stood up. "Y'all had some loose boards on the porch.
Some of them were in bad shape. Thought it'd be a good idea to

change them."

"You don't have to work on stuff here all the time," Wendy said. "You can just come over here and see me."

"Just thought I'd help."

"I just want you to come see me," Wendy said. "Not be my handyman."

Lane put down the hammer he was holding and put his hands in his pocket. He didn't say anything, just kind of stared at Wendy, which irritated her even more.

"You weren't here," Lane said. "I can stop and finish up tomorrow now that you're here."

"It's not that." Wendy rolled her eyes. "Just–I don't know. We're not helpless."

"I know."

"Do you?"

"Wendy."

She shook her head. "I'm sorry. It's just been a long day. Finish what you were doing. I'll see about supper."

She went inside, making sure to let the screen door slam behind her. She went straight to her bedroom and changed clothes. After brushing her hair, she went to the kitchen and found Granny standing at the stove cooking. Whatever was in the pot smelled good and instantly made her stomach growl.

"How long has he been here?" Wendy asked. She sat down at the kitchen table and started filing her nails.

Granny turned to her. "Lane? A couple hours."

"So what, he just came over and started working on stuff without asking?"

"Seems like that's the way it went. Is something wrong?"

"He shouldn't come over and start doing stuff without asking," Wendy said. "It's our place. We're not helpless."

Granny rolled her eyes and turned back to the stove. "Honey, in my experience, men usually don't do work around the house even if you ask. One comes along that does it on his own accord, you keep him around."

"Still."

"And last I checked, this is my place," Granny said. "If that boy wants to help fix it up, he's more than welcome to. I appreciate it, and you should too."

Wendy tilted her head and felt her cheeks glow red with anger. She had all sorts of things to say, but couldn't get them out. She wanted to yell at everyone. Lane, Granny and anyone else who came around. She knew it was a combination of being tired and a general distrust of the male population, but still. Lane needed to mind his own business. She and Granny didn't need anyone feeling sorry for them.

"He's here for you," Granny said. "That's why he's doing all this, you know."

Wendy got up and stood next to her at the stove. "I know, I know. It's an excuse to come over and see me." She took a spoon and took a sip of the stew Granny was making.

Granny gently grabbed her arm. "No, honey. Not like that. Not what I'm saying at all. If he just wanted to see you, he'd ask you out to eat, to the movies stuff like that. He's not the type of man who's scared to ask a woman out."

"Then what's he doing?"

"Getting in it with you, honey. I don't even think he knows it, but that's what he's doing. Your car is broke, he fixes it. Porch needs some work, he's on it. If you get sick, he's gonna take you to the doctor."

Wendy put down the spoon and crossed her arms, looked at the ground.

"Lane's not just interested in you, honey," Granny said. "He's all in. Arm around you, hand in hand on the road with you. Only question is if you're gonna let him walk beside you."

Wendy kept her eyes on the ground. "It's hard."

Granny wrapped her arms around Wendy and held her tight. Tears started falling down Wendy's cheeks as she buried her face into Granny's neck.

"I know it's hard, honey," Granny said. "I know."

They held each other for a little while. Wendy got even more irritated that she couldn't keep it together, couldn't stop herself from being so emotional.

"Food's ready," Granny said. "Go get Lane."

Wendy walked out to the porch, where Lane was hammering nails into a board. She stood over him. He stopped working and looked up at her. His eyes were bloodshot and his face had about a day's worth of stubble on it, but he was still handsome.

"I'm sorry," she said.

"No worries," Lane replied. "Figured you just had a bad day."

"Yeah, but I didn't have to talk to you like that. I'm just cranky sometimes, I guess."

"It's alright."

"Supper's ready. You hungry?"

"Yes ma'am."

Wendy put out her hand, and Lane took it. She pulled to help him up. After he dusted himself off, Wendy eased herself into his body and rested her head against his chest. Lane wrapped his arms around her and held her, and Wendy felt grateful to be embraced by people that loved her. After a moment they went inside and had supper with Granny, a long meal where they talked and laughed for a long time.

Around eight o'clock Granny told them she was going bed because she was extra tired. Wendy thought the old woman was lying and just wanted to give her time to be alone with Lane, but she'd also noticed Granny forgetting things and repeating some stories. So she was probably telling the truth.

When they were washing dishes, Lane asked to see Wendy's room, and she declined.

"Why not?" he asked.

"I don't know," Wendy replied. "Just not yet."

"Okay."

When the dishes were done, she took Lane by the hand and led him to the living room, where they sat down on the plush green couch against the wall. The sun had set and the lights were out, so they could only see each other's dark forms.

"I'll bet that you are a gentleman," Wendy said. "I'll bet you wouldn't spit or curse in front of me. You'd give me your jacket if it was cold. And you wouldn't take advantage of me here in this dark living room. Am I right?"

"Mostly."

"Then I'm going to kiss you, because I don't think you'll kiss me, you being such a gentleman. Just keep your hands in appropriate places, okay?"

"Yes ma'am."

Wendy leaned over and kissed Lane, then pulled back and looked at him. Her eyes were beginning to adjust to the darkness, and she could see the outline of his chin, his mouth, and his nose. She put her hands on his shoulders and pushed him back and then kissed him some more. They laid there for a long time, holding each other and brushing their lips together. Wendy pressed herself against Lane much too tightly, but his body was warm and hard, and she hadn't been with anyone for a long time.

# Victor

There was a panic in his mind, but no one would have been able to tell it had they been watching him. Victor moved with purpose and decisiveness because the waiting was over. He no longer had to be still or motionless because things were finally moving in his favor. And though he was concerned that he hadn't found what he was looking for, he was sure it would turn up eventually.

He carefully opened and closed every cabinet in the cluttered kitchen. The old man was a slob. Mail was stacked everywhere, piles of paper falling all over the counters. There were some dishes in the sink growing mold and maggots. It made Victor gag in disgust. He wanted to clean the entire house.

The master bedroom and bathroom had already been combed over. There was one other bedroom and a small office left. And the living room, though Victor didn't think the old man would hide anything there. He sighed a little in frustration, because even though he'd known the old man for a long time, Victor didn't have a clue about the way he thought. He'd never tried to understand the old man. He was always waiting and waiting until he could wait no more.

A few hours later Victor had searched the entire house, including small closets and even the crawlspace above the hallway. Nothing. Nothing at all. Just more waiting, more patience and hope that what he desired and deserved would soon be in his grasp. As he locked the back door and got in his car, the panic swelled up again in his chest and throat. Victor sat behind the wheel of the car and breathed deep and slow to stop it.

He drove home, cursing the old man the whole way. Not because he was worried. He wasn't, because he was too smart to have his plans screwed up by the old man. No, he had no concern about that. He was angry because again he had to wait. His gratification was delayed again and again. It was time for Victor to succeed, for his patience to be rewarded.

When he walked in the door his mother was gobbling down some sort of chocolate snack cakes. Cow. She was so fat she could barely move, but she was still eating. Years ago Victor thought she would die from her dietary choices. He'd been wrong.

"Victor, I need you to go to the store for me," his mother said through a mouthful of snack cake. "I need some more of these chocolate cakes and some apple juice."

Victor's blood boiled in his chest but he didn't show it. "Yes, mother. I'll go in a little while."

"Thank you, son."

"You're welcome."

He looked her over one more time. The crumbs on her chest. The wrappers around her feet. The rolls of fat showing through her already loose-fitting dress. She was disgusting. Victor couldn't believe they shared any genes at all. He sighed and went to his bedroom to look over the notes he'd taken on the old man over the years. Sooner or later, he'd find what he was looking for.

# Daryl

Back at Shelley's for the third time in a week. Daryl figured he was going to need cholesterol medicine at his next doctor's visit. But he was addicted to Trisha's smile, the warmth she projected. He could brave the greasy meals and Melissa's irritation if it meant getting to see her. It was an odd feeling, an old feeling, like when he was a teenager. It made his blood flow.

Trisha walked over to him and leaned against the counter. The top she was wearing was cut low, and Daryl could see a lot of her chest. He glanced once or twice but otherwise kept his eyes up. She doodled on a notepad while they talked.

"My boyfriend might be leaving," Trisha said.

"Yeah?"

Trisha nodded. "He's thinking about joining the army."

"The army, huh?"

"Yeah."

"Why?"

"He can't do anything else," Trisha said. "Too dumb to go to college, too lazy to keep a job. Least with the army he can't quit."

"True."

Trisha drew some circles on the notepad. Daryl swirled a fry in ketchup and then popped it in his mouth. He didn't say anything because it seemed like Trisha was leading this conversation.

"I told him he should do it," Trisha said. "We kind of got into a fight."

"About what?"

"Just some stuff. You know how it is."

Daryl didn't, but he nodded. "So you want him to go?"

Trisha shrugged. "I don't care I guess."

"So y'all aren't close?"

She shrugged again. "We used to be. Things change. He was real sweet at first, but lately we fight a lot, and he yells too much. He hasn't hit me or anything, but I don't think he's got anything against hitting women. So if he goes, he goes."

"Sounds like you could do better."

"I think so."

Trisha walked over to a table that was trying to get her attention. Daryl watched her pour a man and woman another glass of tea, chat with them a little and then walked back to the counter. She rolled her eyes and shook her head.

"Anyway, if he goes, I'm gonna have to find a new place to live. Or a new roommate. I can't afford the place by myself."

"Where do you live?" Daryl asked.

"Little white house over on Eagle drive."

"Think I know where it is."

Trisha started folding napkins. "Maybe I can get an apartment or something. I don't know. He's not gone yet, so I'll cross that bridge when I get there."

Daryl listened to Trisha talk about her boyfriend a little more, but mostly tuned it out. He wondered how she could live with someone and care so little about them. But he and Melissa were essentially roommates, so he couldn't talk.

They talked while Daryl finished his food. Trisha was going on about how she was thinking about going to the community college to be a nurse or a social worker. He pretended to pay attention but, really, he was just looking at Trisha. It was shallow. He knew that. His obsession with her body was probably unhealthy. All he wanted to do is put his hands all over her. The small of her back. Her belly. Her thighs. Everywhere. She wasn't just body parts, though. Not to him. Every piece of her he longed to touch was just an extension of her soul, another facet of her heart. He knew it.

So he memorized everything he could see and imagined the rest. Around eight o'clock he left Shelley's and drove home as the sky darkened above him. He whistled along to a song on the radio. When he got home, he went to Dustin's room and sat on the narrow twin bed. Dustin was laying on the floor, flipping through some magazine about big cats.

"How was practice?" he asked.

"Good," Dustin replied. "I hit pretty good."

"Good job. You keeping your elbow up?"

"Yes."

"Alright," Daryl said. "How's the hunt going?"

Dustin looked up at him for a moment. "Pretty good, I guess. Nothing worth mentioning though."

"Okay."

Daryl sat there while Dustin flipped a couple more pages. He liked that the boy was taking an interest in the outdoors and in wildlife. And though there was no chance of the boy finding an actual panther, Daryl was happy he was pursuing a goal with such determination.

"Alright, just wanted to see how your day went," Daryl said. He stood up.

"Okay, Dad."

Daryl paused at the door and looked down at Dustin. "Son, what're you gonna do if you find that panther?"

Dustin looked up at him and shrugged. "Don't know. Guess it'll come to me when I find him."

"You've got that pocket knife I gave you?"

"Yes sir."

"Might need to get you a bigger knife."

Dustin shrugged. Daryl smiled at him and then closed the door. He'd be more worried if he thought the boy was actually going to find a panther. Dustin would be alright.

Daryl took a long shower and got ready for bed. He laid down in bed and read an outdoor magazine until Melissa came in for bed. She smiled at him slightly and then went to the bathroom to get ready for bed. Things had been better between the two of them, but he hadn't brought up the boat lately, either. He put down the magazine.

After a few minutes, Melissa got in the bed. Daryl turned out his lamp and turned toward her. She raised her eyebrows, and he took her into his arms. As they held each other in the dark, Daryl closed his eyes and imagined he was holding Trisha. Melissa wasn't as thin as Trisha, but she'd lost weight the last month. Maybe five to ten pounds. He imagined the soft sounds she made were coming from Trisha, and it made him even more turned on. Later, when they were done, he pictured Trisha lying beside him. He knew it would never happen, but it felt good to think about her in his bed, willing to let him touch her wherever he wished. Melissa stirred beside him, so he reached over and rubbed her back with one hand.

# Melissa

The mosquitoes bit at her neck as Melissa walked down the road toward Lane's trailer. The sun had already disappeared behind the tall pines to the west, but somehow it was still hot.

She looked at the trees and bushes beside the road and noticed how much dust coated them. When was the last time it rained? April? March? At church, rain was on the prayer list every week. Some of the folks at church were farmers and ranchers. They depended on the rain for their livelihood.

She walked around to the back of Lane's trailer, the side that faced the woods, like Dustin had told her. Sure enough, there was a lanky man sitting on a tiny porch, smoking a cigarette. He was good looking, and Melissa found herself wondering what he was doing out here in the middle of nowhere by himself. Maybe he just wanted to get away from the city. That's usually what drew people to Crow Valley. It was what brought Lane's parents here, she remembered. When he noticed her approaching, he put the cigarette out by his foot.

"Hello," Melissa called out.

"Evening."

Melissa walked up the stairs and over to him. She shifted the dish she held to her left and offered her right hand. "I'm Melissa, Dustin's mom."

"Oh." He stood up and took her hand. "Lane."

"It's nice to meet you," Melissa said. "Dustin has told me a lot about you, so I thought I should come down and introduce myself."

"I'm glad you did." Lane gestured to the empty chair beside him and took the dish from Melissa.

"It's tater tot casserole," she said.

"Thank you very much." Lane set the dish on the little wooden table beside him. "It'll be nice to have some real food for once."

"How are your parents doing? We miss seeing them."

"They're good," Lane said. "Traveling around the country, seeing the sights. I talk to them about once a week. I think they worry about me. Probably too much."

"Well, that's what parents do. Worry about their children."

"I suppose."

Melissa waited for a moment to see if Lane wanted to say anything else. He seemed quiet and calm. She could see why Dustin liked him. The cigarette smoke lingered in the air.

"I just wanted to thank you for spending time with Dustin this summer," Melissa said. "I know he's probably been bugging you, but I appreciate you letting him run around down here on your property and talk with you."

"He hasn't bothered me at all."

"Thanks for saying that, but I know how kids can be," Melissa said. "It's hard for him. We live so far out here away from everyone else, and he's got no brothers or sisters. I'm glad you've been here this summer. It's like he's had an older brother."

"He's a good kid."

118

"Was that a weird thing to say?" Melissa asked. "The older brother thing?"

Lane shook his head.

"Sorry if it was." Melissa laughed nervously. "But you know what I mean. It's been good for him to have someone to talk to who's not his parents."

"It's been good getting to know him," Lane said. "You can tell he's been raised well."

"Thank you for saying that."

"Y'all lived here long?" Lane asked.

"We bought the place up the hill about fifteen years ago."

Lane nodded. "Do you want something to drink?"

"No, thank you. I should get going. I just wanted to come down and introduce myself. You've been here for a month, and I hadn't been down. I should be a better neighbor."

"You're fine. I haven't been very neighborly, either."

Melissa stood up. "Well, I'm gonna get going. We need to have you over for supper one night."

"I'd love to do that," Lane replied.

"I'll let you know." Melissa walked down the steps. "And if you ever need anything, let us know."

"I will. And if I can do something for y'all, just holler at me."

"Nice to meet you, Lane."

"You too."

Melissa started walking quickly back toward home. She wasn't in a hurry, but wanted to use the opportunity to burn some calories. Daryl had been more affectionate lately, and she knew part of it was the fact that she'd lost more than ten pounds in the last month. Things hadn't really gotten better between them emotionally, but at least they were connecting physically. Sometimes she felt like a prostitute, just there to keep Daryl's appetite satisfied. But she was in no position to take anything in their relationship for granted. She glanced over her shoulder once and saw Lane taking the casserole inside the trailer.

He seemed like a good man. She wanted to know more about

119

him, but it was easy to see he wasn't much of a talker. Maybe when he came for supper he'd talk more with Daryl around. But she felt like Dustin was safe around him, and that's all she wanted to know. Lane didn't seem creepy or dangerous. She liked him.

When she got home, Melissa made hamburgers for her and Dustin because she knew Daryl wouldn't be home for supper. No matter how well things were going between them in the bedroom, she knew something was wrong. She had no idea where he was on those nights when he didn't come home. But she was afraid to say anything because it might take away their nights together. So she got in bed and waited for Daryl to come home and hold her.

# Dustin

Dustin scooped up a handful of dirt and rubbed it in his hands. He didn't know why, but he'd seen pro baseball players do it. He stood by third base and waited for the next player to come up to bat. He realized years ago that baseball was a game of waiting, patience, and determination. So he stood in the sun and the heat and accepted it as part of the game.

He looked to the stands and saw his mom and dad sitting together in the bleachers. They sat close to one another, acting like nothing was wrong. But he knew better. Something was wrong in their home, a rift Dustin couldn't describe but was there nonetheless. He noticed that his dad was rarely at home now, and he wondered why. His mom had tried to explain it away with work, but Dustin was almost thirteen. Maybe that reason would've worked five years ago. Not now.

Dustin settled into a crouch and waited for the next pitch. The batter was a chubby kid who looked familiar, and he had the look of a slugger. Worn batting gloves, thick forearms, and a scowl. Dustin took a step back and pounded his glove. The pitcher went through his windup and whipped the ball to the catcher. Strike one. Dustin stood up and kicked around some more dirt.

They just sat there in the bleachers, laughing and joking with the other parents like nothing was wrong. Just ignoring the fact that three or four nights a week Daryl didn't get home until nine or ten. Or later. How they just existed in the same room and were never *together*, enjoying one another's company, like they were pretending to at the moment. It pissed him off.

"I'm pissed," Dustin whispered. The third base coach for the other team glanced at him.

The pitcher delivered the ball to the plate again and this time the batter connected. Dustin took a step forward as the aluminum bat pinged loudly. A hard grounder came screaming up the line right at him. He squared up on the ball and put his glove down. The ball glanced off the glove and hit him square in the chest, then dropped to the ground in front of him. He picked it up and fired a strike over to first, just beating the batter.

The crowd started cheering, and Dustin heard his dad yell loudly above them. He turned to the outfield and held up his index and pinkie fingers, signaling that there were now two outs. Trying to ignore his dad screaming encouragement at him, Dustin kicked some dirt and waited for the next pitch.

After the game, Dustin and his parents went for a hamburger at a restaurant near the park called Jim's Burgers. Dustin had suggested Shelley's because he wanted waffles, but his dad said that Jim's Burgers had ice cream, and his mom complained about how Shelley's smelled like grease and cigarettes. The ice cream convinced Dustin.

The three of them sat in a booth in the corner and ate their food quietly. His dad gave him tips about baseball he already knew. Dustin read a sports magazine for kids that offered all kind of advice about how to play baseball better. He'd probably know that if he was around a little more. But Dustin listened quietly and nodded in all the right places. His mother nibbled on the chicken breast from a chicken sandwich and occasionally rubbed his dad's shoulder. Dustin squirmed in his seat at the sight of it.

They went home, and it was too dark to do anything but go to his room. Dustin wanted to talk to Lane and tell him about the baseball game. It was too late, he knew, but he asked his mom anyway. She said no. He went to his room and laid on the floor with his baseball glove, tossing a ball up and down. He thought about where the panther might be hiding and where his dad went every night and if Lane was getting sick of a little kid bothering him. After an hour his arm hurt from throwing the ball so much.

He got out his collection of baseball cards and went through them. The cardboard felt flimsy and slick between his fingers. He liked the way they smelled, too. Every now and then he would lift one to his nose and inhale the musty scent. He picked out three of his favorite cards, two of them players from the Houston Astros. He wasn't sure if Lane was a baseball fan, but he was from Houston. Dustin knew that from talking to him. He was going to give them to Lane tomorrow. He hoped Lane liked them.

# Lane

The dreams weren't as bad when he spent time with Wendy. She was the salve, the medicine that kept him sane. Lane stood in front of his bathroom mirror and splashed on some aftershave that his dad left. It made him smell like an old man, but it was the best he could do.

He walked into his bedroom and started going through his bags. They were still full of clothes he hadn't unpacked. He wanted to find the watch his dad gave him years ago as a high school graduation present. Lane took it everywhere. It was old and looked good. Kind of a lucky charm. He'd been wearing it when he met Christie. As he moved socks around looking for it, he came across a small cloth bag. He knew he shouldn't look but he couldn't help it.

Lane opened the bag and emptied the contents into his hand. Two rings fell out. He held them there for a moment and looked at them. One of them was his, a simple gold band. The other was Christie's, similar to his but with a large diamond on it. He set

Christie's on the dresser and stared at his. He remembered buying it, Christie putting it on his finger at their wedding.

Lane took the rings everywhere, too. He knew it wasn't healthy, but he couldn't help it.

He could feel his pulse in his neck, and his head started throbbing. He put his ring in his pocket and headed to the kitchen. He grabbed a bottle from the top of the fridge and took a long gulp. No need to bother with a glass. He drank and drank as the liquor burned his throat. Pretty soon his legs and arms felt heavy and his mind was full of fog. When the bottle was empty, he let it fall to the floor. He found his keys and staggered to his truck while he could still drive.

# Wendy

Wendy heard Lane's truck outside. She was reading in her room, waiting on him to show up. She was looking forward to going out with him again. He was laid back and fun. Not like a lot of guys she'd dated, always trying to impress her. She put the book down, checked herself in the mirror one last time, then said goodbye to Granny. She walked out to the porch expecting to meet Lane, but when she got there, she saw he was still in the truck.

She waited for a few moments, but after a while she realized Lane wasn't getting out. He was just sitting there, head against the seat and staring up at the ceiling of the truck. Wendy walked over and stood by the door. Lane didn't acknowledge her, only kept looking at the ceiling. She knocked on the window, which got his attention. He looked at her like he was surprised to see her standing there. The window rolled down.

"Hey," Lane said. "How you doing?"

Wendy could smell the liquor immediately. It was worse than usual. Much worse. Lane's eyes were red and glazed. She sighed.

"What are you doing?" she asked.

Lane looked confused. "Thought we were going out for a bite."

"We were."

"Alright then."

Wendy opened the door. "Get out of the truck."

Lane looked at her and then looked at the ground. He slowly lowered himself out of the truck and then took two staggering steps before he was able to stand up straight.

"God, I have the worst taste in men," Wendy said. She shut the truck door and then put her arm around Lane's waist. She guided him up the porch stair and into the living room, where she deposited him on the couch.

"Thanks," he said.

"Shut up."

Wendy took off his boots. Lane murmured something and closed his eyes. She considered slapping him awake but didn't. She watched him for a few moments, then rolled her eyes and went back to her room. Granny ran into her in the hallway and looked surprised.

"Aren't you supposed to be out with Lane?" Granny asked.

"Yes." Wendy gestured to the living room. "But he's in no shape to go anywhere."

"What?"

Wendy took her by the arm and showed her Lane. Granny clucked and shook her head. They left him there on the couch and went to the kitchen.

"He drove over here like that?" Granny asked.

Wendy nodded.

"Shame."

"What am I doing Granny? I'm right back where I was, making stupid decisions and falling for the wrong guys. Nothing different."

"Just stay calm, honey," Granny said. "You're angry and upset, and you have a right to be. Let him sleep it off, and you two figure it out in the morning."

"Let him sleep it off? There's nothing to figure out."

"Honey, he's going through something bad. We all do sometimes. You need to decide if you're willing to go through it with him."

Wendy crossed her arms and walked over to a window. She stared at the small grove of trees behind their house. The trees weren't very tall, just high enough to provide a little shade for the pond they surrounded.

"Why do I keep doing this?" she asked.

Granny didn't answer. She walked over and rubbed Wendy's back. Wendy leaned back while Granny wrapped her arms around her. It felt safe and reminded her of when she was little and Granny would hold her.

"Just wait until morning and talk to...the boy. Him. What's his name?"

"Lane."

"Right. Lane. Talk to him in the morning and see what he says."

"Okay."

Granny hugged her tightly and then went to her bedroom. Wendy walked to the living room and watched Lane sleeping on the couch. His long, lanky frame stretched out like he was relaxed, but his face looked concerned and angry. She wondered what he was dreaming about.

# Victor

He could hear his mother snoring while he organized his things. All the photographs of insects and arachnids he had dissected over the years. The mice and cats and dogs as well. People often remarked that there were very few stray animals in Crow Valley, as if they had something to do with keeping the town clean and vibrant. Victor did the dirty work for them. He made sure their hands were white as snow while his were stained crimson.

He placed the photographs in a large wooden box and locked it with a small padlock. He picked it up and carried it outside to the metal shed in the backyard. Once inside the pristine shed, he placed the box on a table beside a few similar boxes. He stepped back and stared at them, satisfied with his work.

As he looked over the boxes, he began to see an image in his mind. At first he was angry with himself for not realizing sooner, but the rapture of the knowledge soon melted away any rage he might have felt. In the old man's shed was a table full of junk. In the corner, covered by a sheet, was a large metal box. A safe. Victor knew it because once he had bumped his elbow on it. He was busy at the time, so he thought nothing of it. But looking back now, it's was the only place the safe could be.

Victor walked quickly from the shed. Didn't even bother locking it. He grabbed his keys from his pocket and headed for his car. It would be suspicious if someone saw him at the old man's house this time of night. But that didn't matter. He was tired of waiting. Tired of being patient. And now he was so close to his goal. Close to his salvation.

He put the key in the ignition and turned it. The car made a sputtering sound and failed to start. Victor tried it again. Same result. He popped the hood and looked at the engine. He didn't see anything obviously wrong. He got in the car and tried the key again. Same sputtering sound. Victor cursed loudly and then screamed as he kicked his car over and over again.

# Daryl

Daryl leaned over the desk and stared at the floor plans for the apartments. He needed a two bedroom, because Dustin would be staying with him on weekends. It was important that the boy had a place to feel at home when he was staying with Daryl. Also important was staying within his budget. The house was paid off, so it would be easy for Melissa to live on the child support he'd be sending. He was hoping that neither of them would be put out financially when the time came to separate.

This was the sixth complex he'd tried. Two had been within his budget but looked like they were crawling with rats and bugs. The other three had been nice but way more than he was able to pay. He was hoping that this one, The Stonewood Apartments, would be the right fit. It was an older complex, but looked like it was well maintained.

The woman across from him, Erica, was attractive. In fact, every leasing agent he'd spoken with had been an attractive female dressed in business casual clothes that were slightly revealing. This one was a redhead with milky white skin and hypnotizing green eyes. Her neck was very long and elegant. Daryl wanted to kiss it and couldn't help staring. He was distracted, probably not good when making a financial decision.

"Okay, this two bedroom, two bath is six fifty a month," Erica said. "There's a two hundred dollar deposit and a fifty dollar application fee. You get the deposit back when you move out, but the application fee is non-refundable, even if you don't qualify for a lease. Any questions?"

"No, not that I can think of," Daryl replied. "How much for a three bedroom?"

"Our least expensive three bedroom is eight fifty a month. Do you want to see one?"

Daryl cocked his head to the side and considered it. "No, I better not. That's a little outside of my budget. I better just stick with the two bedroom."

"Okay, let me just grab the keys and we'll go look."

Over the next thirty minutes they toured two different floor plans for two bedroom, two bath apartments. Daryl preferred the one with the bigger dining room. He planned on having a table to eat off of. He wasn't going to be one of those bachelors that ate in front of the TV every night.

They went back to the office and talked about some more details. Daryl wasn't ready to commit yet, which prompted some high pressure sales tactics from Erica. She let him know that the unit might not be available in a week. Touched his hand quite a bit and let him know that it would be great to have him in the community. He told her there were circumstances that didn't allow him to sign the lease just yet. He didn't say it was his wife.

Daryl took a folder full of informational brochures from Erica and thanked her for her time. Stonewood was the best fit so far. He'd probably end up there. He wasn't concerned about units being available. Someone was always moving out of an apartment. He would wait and make sure that he had a unit leased before he broke the news to Melissa.

When he got home he did some work out in his shed. He enjoyed doing woodwork and had started making that table for his future dining room. If Melissa asked about it, he would say it was for their dining room here at the house. But she rarely came out to the shed so he didn't think he'd have to craft that lie. Daryl hadn't told her he'd taken the day off to look at apartments. How could he? She would have thrown a fit. Not that he'd blame her.

He'd been lying to Melissa their whole marriage, but recently it had picked up considerably. Most of them were lies of omission, but he'd always been taught those were just as bad. He didn't like doing it. He couldn't see any other option, though. God, what would it look like if everyone told their spouses the truth one hundred percent of the time? The truth was that it seemed near impossible for two people to get along all the time for the rest of their lives. And telling someone what you were thinking all the time was a good way to end a marriage early.

Later that night, Melissa came to bed and reached for him, pressed her body against him. He took off her clothes, then his, and held her. He closed his eyes and imagined she was Erica, with the long, elegant neck and beautiful red hair. Another lie of omission. After they were done, Daryl left Melissa sleeping in bed and went to the porch. He called Trisha, and they talked until two in the morning.

# Melissa

S omething startled Melissa and woke her from a deep sleep. Her
eyes shot open and she looked to her right. Daryl was gone. She
got out of bed and dressed. She walked through the house
searching for him. Something was wrong. That was why she
woke so suddenly. She wasn't sure what was going on, but she had to
find Daryl.

In the living room, she heard soft talking coming from the
porch. At first she was scared and thought there were intruders on
the porch. Then she realized she was hearing Daryl's voice and
calmed down. She approached the window and listened carefully.

He was on the phone. Talking with a woman. She knew it,
though she couldn't say why. It was the way his voice had a higher
inflection, a sweeter tone. She knew it because he had talked to her
that way once. A long time ago. Her fingers started tingling and her
face flushed. She could feel her heart beating in her chest. It took
every bit of willpower she had not to throw the lamp near her

through the window.

Melissa listened for a little longer and then went back to bed. She laid there, staring at the ceiling, crying hard. Sobs kept rising in her chest and she fought them back. She didn't want him to know she knew. She would deal with it in the morning, when Daryl was at work. She needed the night to work things out. To understand the situation. To decide whether she wanted to kick him out or simply kill him.

# Dustin

Lane wasn't home when Dustin stopped by. His truck was gone, so Dustin put the baseball cards in his pocket and started for the woods. It was early in the morning and the ground was still wet with dew. He couldn't imagine where Lane might be this early. Since Dustin had known him, Lane had never been an early riser. In fact, Dustin wondered if Lane ever slept at all. Maybe he had errands to run.

Dustin had wanted to leave the house as soon as possible. The mornings had been tense lately, but today was terrible. His parents barely looked at each other. It was worse than when they were fighting before the summer started. Now things just simmered all over, and he hated it. It felt like a fuse had been lit in his home and he didn't know when the dynamite was going to explode.

Dustin headed toward the eastern part of the woods, a place he hadn't yet searched. It was where the small creek emptied into Crow Creek, which was larger and flowed into the Trinity River.

There were some low hills there. He hoped to find the highest and look around. See if he could spot anything interesting. The only problem is that it would take him at least an hour, maybe two to get to the area. And the same amount of time walking back. It would cut down on the time he could actually search. But maybe that's where the panther was.

Even though he was used to it, the heat was tremendous. It hadn't rained since March. He was sure of it. The rain was becoming legendary, a myth. Some people claimed it had rained in May. Others said it hadn't rained since January. Either way, people were starting to talk about it with desperation in their voices, like starving people talk about food. Dustin's family wasn't affected by it, he knew that. His dad was a game warden, and his salary didn't vary based on the weather. But a lot of people at church raised cattle, cut hay, and grew cotton for a living. And the empty skies and dry earth were ruining them. They talked about it at church, prayed, and begged Jesus for a little precipitation.

One of his friends on the baseball team, Ricky, had said the preacher at his church told the congregation that the drought was a punishment from God. He was trying to get America to repent for their sins, like nudity in movies and people gambling in Oklahoma. Dustin didn't know if that was true, but it seemed wrong of God to punish the people of Crow Valley for gambling and nudity in movies. Dustin didn't know anyone that gambled, and they definitely didn't make movies here. Why wasn't Hollywood dry as a bone if that was the case?

All he knew was God didn't want Crow Valley to get rain anymore.

After about an hour, Dustin found the tallest hill in the woods, which was simply a big pile of dirt with grass on it. But it provided a good view of the creek below, which wound through the woods like a giant snake made of water. It was a beautiful view, even if the grass around him was turning yellow from lack of rain. He followed the creek with his eyes, where it emerged from the deep woods into the clearing below him.

137

About a hundred yards from where the small creek met Crow Creek, in a bend, was a severed deer leg lying by the water. Dustin's heart started racing. He ran down the hillside as fast he could without falling. It took him about five minutes of maneuvering over fallen tree branches and thorn bushes to reach it. The banks near the bend were at least ten feet high. Dustin eyed the best path down, then climbed down the steep bank.

Using tree roots as foot holds, he carefully descended. But only a foot down, one of the roots was rotten and broke. He slipped and lost any kind of grip to the bank and slid down. He started rolling quickly and didn't stop until he hit the bottom the creek bank. There was a blackberry bush near the creek and he landed in it. The tiny thorns scratched at his skin and it stung badly. Dustin rolled to his right to get out of the bush and then laid on his back, looking up at the sky in pain.

At the top of the bank where he had just been standing was the panther. It looked down at him with its yellow eyes. Its face looked curious, as if he wasn't quite sure what Dustin was. From farther away, it looked sleek and thin. But Dustin remembered when he was closer how its muscles rippled and the power in its growl.

Dustin was afraid to move at all. He barely took a breath as the panther watched him. Waiting for something. For a second Dustin thought maybe the panther didn't see him. But it did. He was looking into Dustin's eyes. Sniffing the air to catch his scent. And now the question that Lane had asked popped into his mind. *What are you gonna do when you find this panther?*

Here he was, staring at what he'd been searching for, what had consumed him for more than a month. His camera was in his backpack, still strapped to his back. He didn't dare try to get it, though. The panther didn't take its eyes off of Dustin, who had no idea what reaction any kind of movement might cause. So he stayed still as a rock, locking eyes with the panther.

After about a minute, the panther let loose a low growl and slowly loped away. Dustin laid by the creek for a long time, breathing rapidly. His head felt like it was about to explode and his skin burned from the scratches left by the blackberry bush. He kept his eyes on the top of the creek bank, waiting to see if the panther would return. It didn't.

He stood up and looked at his arms. They were bleeding from a hundred tiny scratches. Dustin ignored the deer leg. It didn't matter anymore. He followed the creek back toward Lane's house, walking through it where it was shallow enough. He cupped some water in his hands and rubbed it on the scratches on his arms. The cold water felt good.

When he got home, his mom was pretty upset about the scratches. She put alcohol onto a cotton ball and rubbed it on his skin. The scratches were on his arms and back mostly. A few on his legs. He wondered if any of them would scar up. Probably not. None of them were deep. He didn't tell his mom about the panther. He wasn't going to tell anyone except Lane.

# Lane

The darkness was interrupted by a severe stinging on his cheek. Lane opened his eyes to Wendy standing over him and slapping his face. Everything was blurry and his head ached. He felt nauseated. Wendy slapped his cheek again. Things cleared up a little. He raised himself up and rubbed his eyes.

"You awake?" Wendy asked.

"A little."

"I'll bring you some water and aspirin."

Wendy disappeared into the kitchen. Lane swung his feet onto the floor and sat with his head in his hands for a while. The world was spinning, and his stomach flopped inside him. When Wendy returned, he took the aspirin and gulped the water as fast as he could, then asked for another glass. Wendy went to the kitchen again and came back with water. She sat beside him on the couch while he sipped it.

"We need to talk," Wendy said.

"Figured."

"Put your shoes on and we'll take a walk." Wendy turned her head away. "There's some mouthwash in the bathroom. You should use it."

Lane put his shoes on and went to the bathroom while Wendy waited on the porch. He splashed some water on his face and used the spearmint flavored mouthwash. He looked at himself in the mirror. His eyes were really red, his cheeks sagged and there were dark circles under his eyes. He cursed at himself and then went to meet Wendy.

"Come with me," Wendy said. She grabbed his hand and led him around to the back of her house. From there she took him onto a trail that led up a hill just north of the house. They walked until they reached the top of the hill.

"My grandpa and Granny used to own a hundred acres here," Wendy said. "Starting at the road there and going back to the east. Used it to grow things, raise cattle, stuff like that. Over the years they sold off parts of it. Now we're down to less than twenty."

Wendy leaned her head on his shoulder. Even though he felt like he was in the doghouse, Lane put his arm around her shoulders.

"He was always there for her, always ready to do anything she needed done. And when I was fourteen, my parents died, and he was there for me. I watched him, how he loved Granny and me, until he died four years ago. So I know what a man looks like. I know how a man treats a woman he loves. I've seen it with my own eyes."

"I know I messed up, Wendy. I understand what you're saying."

"No, you don't."

"No, I get it."

"I know you're like my grandpa," Wendy said. "Granddaddy is what I called him. I see it in your eyes. I know it in my heart. But you've got this weight on your shoulders, something you're bearing. And I know from experience that I can't make it go away. I might distract you from it for a while, but I can't get rid of it. That's between you and God and whoever hurt you. But underneath all that, you're a good man. I know that like I know the sun will come up over those trees tomorrow."

Lane's eyes started watering. No one called him a good man.

"I can't be with you if that burden's bigger than me," Wendy said. "I'm not asking you to change. I'm just asking to be the most important thing on your mind when you wake up. That's what you'll be to me."

Lane didn't speak, couldn't speak. He grabbed Wendy's shoulders and looked at her and simply nodded. He pulled her close and hugged her tightly. After a moment, she gently pushed him away.

"Don't say anything," she said. "I don't want to hear any romantic speeches or promises you can't keep. I've never wanted to live in a crappy romance novel. Just think about what I said, and we'll take this thing day by day."

Lane nodded. She grabbed his hand.

"Let me show you the rest of our property," she said.

They walked across fields starting to brown from lack of rain. Wendy showed him the tree house her grandpa built for her and her cousins. She took him to the very back of the property and showed him the horses raised by the neighbors. They walked through the woods where Wendy played hide and seek as a child and stopped at a beautiful pond. It was much clearer than most country ponds. Lane could see the bottom. It was deep and had a lot of rocks in it.

"There's a spring at the bottom," Wendy said. "That's why it's so clear. My grandpa put the rocks in, so the bottom isn't so slimy."

"It's beautiful."

"I love it."

They stood beside each other, holding hands. Lane leaned over and kissed Wendy's cheek. She looked up at him and smiled.

"What happened to your parents?" Lane asked.

"They were in a car wreck. I was staying here for a couple weeks. It was summer."

Lane looked at the ground. "I'm sorry."

Wendy smiled at him and then looked away. Lane walked down to the pond and stood by the water. He turned and looked at

Wendy, who had sat down on the grass.

"It's cold water, right?" he asked.

She nodded her head and looked confused.

"Let's jump in."

"What?"

"C'mon."

Lane was tired of the heat and the dry earth and the sand. He stripped down to his boxers and waded into the pond. It was cold and wet and felt good on his skin. He waded out until the water was waist deep.

"What are you doing?" Wendy called from shore.

"Cooling off. Get in."

Wendy shook her head and laughed. She walked down closer to the water and stood with her arms crossed.

"No way."

"Get in." Lane splashed some water at her. "It feels good."

Wendy laughed and her face turned red. "That's okay. I'll just stay here and enjoy the view."

Lane smiled at her and then turned. He waded farther into the pond and then laid back into the water and sank. Let the water wash over him and wash the sweat and dirt away. Wash away all the filth from yesterday until he was clean. When he came out of the water, he saw Wendy sitting on the grass. She smiled and waved. Just the sight of her made something inside him twinge, break, and pour out. He felt the tears coming so he ducked back under the water so she wouldn't see him cry. Covered by the clear, cool water he sobbed and didn't know why.

He knew, though, that Wendy was his only hope, his only chance to live again. He didn't know if they would be together forever or even for a year but he knew he could survive if he ran to her with recklessness and abandon. And now he just wanted her to hold him. She could take his hurt, and he would take hers until they were both well enough to stand on their own again.

Lane came up for air and gulped hard at the fresh oxygen. He waded back over to Wendy and sat down beside her. Water dripped off of him and for once the sun felt good on his back. Wendy kept her eyes straight ahead but smiled.

"Was starting to worry about you," she said.

"Haven't been swimming in a while."

Lane reached out and gently turned Wendy's face toward him and kissed her. She kissed him back. After a moment, she pushed him back.

"You should put your clothes on," she said. "Don't want Granny to see you like this. She's got a gun somewhere."

Lane dressed by a tree. He and Wendy walked hand in hand back to the house and spent the rest of the day on the porch, reading books and mixing in the occasional kiss.

# Victor

It took all night, but Victor got his car running by late morning. His hands were greasy and full of scrapes from hitting his knuckles on metal. That's what happened when you rushed. But now there was no time. Victor usually waited and waited. Always patient. With his goal so close, though, he had to hurry.

He sped over to the old man's house and went straight to the shed. At the back, amid all the junk, was a large square object covered by a dusty old sheet. Victor carefully removed all the other junk from the table and then removed the sheet. Just as he thought, a large metal safe sat there. It was about four feet wide by three feet high. It was bigger than he thought and he wondered how he could have missed it. Probably because of the mountain of junk the old man kept around it.

There was a combination lock on the safe, which actually made Victor smile. The old man wasn't smart and was such a creature of habit that Victor already knew the combination. For any kind of password or code, the old man always used his birthday. He was always proud about being born on Independence Day in 1928. Victor punched the combination into the number pad on the outside of the safe and felt his heart leap when the light on it turned green. Victor turned the metal handle and opened the door.

But all that opened was an outer door. Inside, there was another lock. A key lock. And Victor had no key. He felt dizzy and nauseated and needed to sit down. He fell to his knees and tried to fight the panic. All was not lost, but he'd made a mistake. Victor looked to the sky and screamed with anguish.

He knew where the key was.

# Wendy

Wendy and Lane fell asleep on a blanket in the yard behind the house. He held her tight as they lay in the shade while the afternoon sun shone down hard on the parched earth.

She dreamed of her parents and a home of her own and lying on beaches with Lane while they forgot about time.

At some point Lane woke up and kissed her on the forehead. He left, and she wanted to call out to him to stay but was in such a deep fog of sleep she couldn't. He faded away into darkness as her eyelids fell down heavy. Wendy curled into a ball and dreamed again. Even when he was away she felt safe.

She woke later in the evening, when the sky was glowing purple and the mosquitoes were beginning to prick at her skin. She rolled up the blanket and wondered where Lane had gone and why she was so tired.

# Victor

Victor had pulled his car off to the side of the tiny dirt road and turned on his hazard lights. If anyone asked him what was wrong, he would just tell them his car had a coolant system problem and he was waiting for it cool down. He crept off the road, stepping over brush and the occasional prickly pear until he reached the barbed wire fence that sat five feet away from the road.

He carefully stood by the fence, hidden by the oak trees that grew there. He was on top of a hill that looked down on a large field that slowly became a thick forest of pine trees. Near the edge of the forest was a small trailer house. When he had been here before, there was no one at the trailer. Now there was a pickup truck parked outside.

The key had been on a chain around the old man's neck. Victor remembered it very well. He'd noticed it when he had his hands around the old man's neck, squeezing until his face turned

148

blue. Victor cursed loudly for not thinking it was valuable, for not taking care of every single detail.

He watched as a young boy emerged from the woods and walked past the trailer. Victor felt the pulse in his neck quicken. The boy walked up the dirt road, probably to the house Victor had passed on his way here. Victor got in his car and went home, cursing men and gods all the way.

# Daryl

aryl parked his truck beside the house and killed the engine. He sighed loudly. He didn't want to go inside. There was something inside his chest, something like a sob that wanted to come out, and he couldn't release it or make it go away. More than that, he was tired. He was tired of seeing this beautiful woman he wanted to touch but couldn't. He was tired of pretending to be a husband. He was exhausted.

He got out of the truck and went inside. Melissa was cleaning up the kitchen and didn't acknowledge him. He was later than usual. Time had gotten away from him while talking to Trisha. But Melissa didn't seem to care. Daryl changed clothes and then stopped by Dustin's room.

Dustin had fallen asleep on the floor with encyclopedias and magazines and books lying all around him. Daryl smiled. He thought this fascination with the panther would go away, but it had stuck. The boy was determined, and Daryl appreciated that. He picked Dustin

150

up, set him on his bed and put the sheet over him. He watched his son sleeping there for a minute and then turned out the lights and shut the door. The boy deserved better than Daryl. He deserved someone who didn't have his mind somewhere else whenever he was home.

Daryl walked to the bedroom and got undressed. He laid down in bed, turned on his side and stared out the window into the darkness.

# Melissa

Melissa sat on the porch and stared out into the night. Usually she would read a devotional by porch light, but she was too angry and sad for that. Right here, in this chair, her husband was talking to another woman by phone. She didn't want to think about what he was doing when he was gone.

She stayed out there for hours, long after Daryl and Dustin had gone to bed. She thought of her whole life and everything that she and Daryl had built. The house she lived in, the cars they drove and all the memories they'd made. They all seemed rotten and decayed now. It was like she could feel her home falling apart, turning into dust and ashes beneath her very feet.

After midnight Melissa went to bed. She laid there beside Daryl and fought the urge to cry. After a minute she reached for him. She wondered if he imagined the other woman while they had sex and just thinking about that made her hate him and whoever the woman was. She wanted to kill him. But she wanted to see it in his eyes. She wanted to see him close his eyes and picture her as someone else.

Daryl turned to her and she kissed him deeply. He returned it, and she waited for him to pull her into him. But he didn't. He looked up at her like he was confused. Melissa waited, didn't say anything. They stared into each other's eyes for a few moments, saying nothing, like they did when they were younger. There was none of that youthful passion here, though, no love bursting through their eyes. They just studied each other like two animals.

"Not tonight," Daryl whispered. "It's been a long day."

Melissa nodded. He kissed her and turned away. Melissa got out of bed and dressed, putting on a tank top, shorts, and sandals. She quietly slipped out the door and walked down the road to Lane's trailer. It was darker than she thought it would be. The half-moon shone down some light, but there were clouds.

As she approached the trailer, she saw Lane was on the porch smoking a cigarette. He noticed her but didn't acknowledge her. He just followed her with his eyes. She walked up the steps and sat down beside him.

"I'm hospitable, but it's awfully late," Lane said. "Everything alright?"

"Sorry. I just needed to get some air."

"Is there something I can do for you?"

Melissa nodded toward the bottle of whiskey near his feet. "I could use some of that."

"You drink?"

"Yes."

Lane shrugged his shoulders and went inside the trailer. He came back with two glasses and handed one to Melissa. She held it with both hands. He opened the bottle and poured a little into her glass. She sniffed the whiskey and took a sip. She hadn't had any kind of liquor since college. The whiskey burned her throat.

"Most folks would think it's inappropriate for a married woman to be drinking alone with a man this late at night."

"Are you most folks?" Melissa asked.

"No, ma'am."

She took a long drink of the whiskey and then coughed. "I don't think I'll be married much longer, so it doesn't matter."

Lane flicked his cigarette and cut his eyes away from her. "I don't know if I'm the one you should be talking to about that."

"I'm sorry."

Lane took a sip of his drink. Melissa felt bad being here with him, making him feel awkward. But she couldn't be under the same roof as Daryl. Not right now.

"I'm sorry," Lane said. "I don't mean to be rude."

"I need to stay. For a while. I won't talk about it, I promise. Please."

Lane sighed and nodded. He took a long drink from his glass. Melissa did the same. Her arms were starting to feel heavy.

"Thank you," she said.

They sat on the porch and sipped the whiskey for a long time. They made small talk and Melissa kept her promise. She didn't bring up Daryl once. Mostly she talked about Dustin, which seemed to make Lane happy.

"Do you do this every night?" Melissa asked. "Sit out here like this?"

"Most nights."

"Why?"

"Helps me think," Lane said. "I have trouble sleeping."

"Me too." Melissa held out her glass and Lane poured her some whiskey. "Don't know why."

"So were you gonna knock on my door and ask for a drink, even if I was asleep?"

"Yes."

Lane raised his eyebrows.

"I had to get out of the house," Melissa said. "I knew you had something to drink. I needed a drink."

"I think this is where I'm supposed to tell you." Lane tapped his glass. "That this doesn't solve any problems."

"Helps you forget."

"True."

"Do you want me to leave?" Melissa asked. "So you can sleep?"

"No."

"No?"

"I should probably tell you to go," Lane said. "But I'm not going to go to sleep. I usually don't."

Melissa didn't say anything. They just sat on the porch, drinking, staring into the woods until sunlight started emerging from behind the pine trees. A few deer stood near the edge of the woods grazed. Melissa stood and kissed Lane on the forehead. She walked down the porch steps and started toward her house. She stopped in front of Lane.

"You mind if I take that?" she asked, pointing at the bottle of whiskey.

"Go ahead," Lane replied. "I'm trying to quit, anyway."

Melissa grabbed the bottle and started to walk away. She stopped again and looked up at Lane.

"We're going to see the fireworks on Monday," she said. "You wanna come with us?"

Lane looked down at her and smiled. "Can I bring a date?"

"Wendy?"

He nodded.

"Bring her along. Should be fun."

# Dustin

The whole town came out for the fireworks. It was the best day in Crow Valley every year. At least that's what Dustin thought. He didn't like the parade, which was mostly old guys in shiny old cars. But there was a fair and then the fireworks. There was so much food and lights and rides. Best of all, he got to see a lot of his friends that he hadn't seen since school let out.

And this year was even better, because Lane was with them. Wendy, too, though he didn't care if she came or not. She was pretty, sure, but she didn't care about hunting panthers or spitting or shooting guns. Lane and Wendy had joined Dustin and his parents for supper at Dairy Queen. After hamburgers and ice cream, they'd headed over to the park where all the activities were going on.

They walked around, played some games, and ate a funnel cake. Dustin rode a small Ferris wheel but it wasn't very fun. Now his parents and Lane and Wendy had spread blankets on the ground by the soccer fields, where everyone was gathering to watch the fireworks. The sky was beginning to turn black and the stars were just beginning to twinkle. The adults sat there talking to one another. Lane and his dad were talking about hunting. Wendy and his mom were talking about the beach. Both conversations were boring to him.

Dustin tapped his mom on the shoulder. "Mom, can I go ride the spinning thing?"

"What?"

"That one with the yellow and orange lights that spins you around fast," Dustin said. "Can I go ride it?"

His mom bit her lip and then looked over at Daryl. He stopped talking to Lane and then shrugged his shoulders.

"Okay, you can go," she said. "Do you have enough tickets?"

"Yes, ma'am."

"Be careful."

Dustin nodded and started running toward the rides. He wove through all kinds of people, waving at the people he recognized. He didn't stop to talk with them though. All the food he'd eaten weighed heavy on his stomach and he felt like he might throw up. But he didn't slow down. He wanted to get on the ride and get back to see the fireworks.

The line at the spinning thing, which was actually called the Whirly-Go, was short. People were beginning to drift away to watch the fireworks. Dustin stood in line patiently until the ride stopped and emptied out. He and five other people got on the ride after giving their tickets to the attendant. It left Dustin with two tickets, enough to buy a soda.

He settled into a seat by himself and looked around. There were bright lights and music and smells. It overwhelmed his senses, and he loved it. He glanced at his fellow riders and noticed one of them was Becky Roberts. She must have jumped on the ride at the last minute because he hadn't noticed her in line. She waved at him. Dustin waved back and tried to act casual. He looked away when he realized he was blushing.

The ride started and spun him around until the world was a blur of carnival lights and darkness. His stomach lurched, and it felt

157

like food was in his throat. But he fought with all of his might to hold back any vomit. He didn't want Becky Roberts seeing something that embarrassing.

When the ride was over, he staggered out the exit of the ride a little dizzy. Becky was standing just outside the ride, waiting for him. Dustin straightened up and tried to act like the ride hadn't affected him. Keeping food down was taking up most of his focus at the moment. He decided he would just say little. Girls probably liked that.

"Hey!" Becky called to him.

Dustin walked over to her. "Hey."

"Fun ride, huh?"

Dustin swallowed hard and nodded. Doing pretty good.

"How long you been here?" she asked.

"A few hours."

"I've been here pretty much all day."

"Cool."

"What've you been doing this summer?" Becky asked.

"Nothing much really." Dustin didn't want to tell her he'd spent most of every day looking for a panther that he was mostly sure existed. "Playing baseball some. What about you?"

"Me and my family went to Disney World a couple weeks ago. But other than that, I've just been hanging out."

"Cool."

"Yeah."

They stood there together and didn't say anything. Becky kept looking at him and it made Dustin think he was supposed to do something. Luckily his stomach had stopped doing back flips. Sort of.

"You looking forward to the fireworks?" Becky asked.

"Yeah."

"Me too."

Dustin shoved his hands in his pockets because it gave him something to do. In his right pocket, he felt the tickets he had left. He'd forgotten all about them. Now that his stomach was feeling better, he was thirsty.

"Do you wanna get a drink?" he asked Becky.

"Yes."

"C'mon."

They walked quickly over to a concession stand and stood in line. The people ahead of them ordered nachos and pickles and barbecue sandwiches. Dustin looked up at the sky. It was almost completely black now. The fireworks would start soon.

"Do you have any tickets?" he asked.

Becky shook her head. "No."

"I've only got two. We can only get one drink, but we can share, if you don't mind."

"That's fine."

"We can get two straws," Dustin said.

"Okay."

They ordered a Dr Pepper and got two straws. Becky suggested they go sit at a picnic table by the baseball field. They sat on the table and took turns sipping out of the Styrofoam cup while they talked about which teachers they wanted next year. The baseball field was dark but the glow from the carnival lit it up just enough to see the brown grass and red dirt. To Dustin it looked haunted.

"Have you heard about the scoreboard?" Becky asked.

Dustin looked at the scoreboard standing just above the fence in centerfield. It looked normal enough to him. It was a little big for a high school baseball field, but other than that he didn't know what she was talking about.

"What?"

"There's a catwalk on the back of it, and the trees back there hide it," Becky said. "It's where the high school kids go to make out."

"Really?"

"Yup." Becky took a sip. "No one can see you up there."

"Huh."

Becky played with her straw for little bit. "Do you wanna go look at it?"

"Why?"

"See if anyone's there."

"Maybe."

"Or just to see it."

Dustin wanted to see the fireworks. They were set to start any minute. But being alone with Becky Roberts somewhere dark and private appealed to him. He looked over at her and felt his stomach flip again, but this time it felt good. Her light brown hair framed her chubby cheeks and expecting eyes.

"Let's go."

They drained the rest of the Dr Pepper and ran across the baseball field. They headed toward the right field foul pole, where there was a gate that opened to a path that led behind the outfield wall. Dustin heard a loud sound, like a gun. He turned and looked up at the sky. A tiny red flame was rising among the stars. They were shooting flares off to test the wind. The fireworks would start soon.

Becky was right. Behind the centerfield scoreboard was a metal catwalk. Probably put there for repairs. They stood there staring at it like it was Mount Rushmore or the Grand Canyon, some natural wonder made by God himself. Dustin grabbed Becky's hand.

"Let's climb it."

After he said it he was instantly embarrassed and glad it was dark so Becky couldn't see his face turning red. But he liked climbing things and he liked Becky, so it seemed like a good idea. Becky didn't hesitate at all. She followed him to the ladder descending from the catwalk. Dustin grabbed the first rung he could reach and climbed as fast as he could. Halfway up, he looked down. Becky was climbing just as fast.

They reached the top just as the fireworks started. Explosions thundered above them and the sky turned red and green and purple. The colors lit up their faces and somehow it made Becky look even prettier than before. The catwalk looked over a small grove of pine and cedar trees that grew just beyond the centerfield fence. It blocked their view of the soccer fields that lay just beyond the trees, but it also shielded them from anyone else.

"It's like our own fireworks show," Dustin said.

Becky nodded but didn't take her eyes off the fireworks in

the sky. Dustin stared at her and felt his heart beat faster. He could see the fireworks reflecting in her eyes. And for some reason, as he looked into her eyes, he thought of the panther he had seen and its glowing yellow eyes. His heart skipped a beat again, but this time it was fear. He was scared the panther had followed him here and hid in the woods waiting to kill him. That was stupid, though. Dustin knew it. The panther did not care about him at all.

He thought about telling Becky about the panther. She wouldn't make fun of him and wouldn't think he was lying or making up a story. Becky would believe him. He knew it, somehow, just like he knew he would see the panther again. And knowing that she believed him, trusted him and wanted to be alone with him made him love her. At least he thought it was love. Whatever feeling was swelling up in his chest right now felt like love, what all the books and movies and songs said was love. So he gently turned her toward him and kissed her on the lips. His knees trembled.

It wasn't difficult or awkward. It felt like the only thing in the world to do. And Becky kissed him back. She didn't pull away or slap him or anything. They pressed their lips together and stayed that way for a few seconds. Her lips were so soft. She put her hand on his cheek and then they separated.

A shy smile spread across Becky's face and then she looked down. Dustin looked up at the sky and looked at the fireworks. They might as well be inside his heart.

He stayed there with Becky, holding her hand, until the fireworks stopped. They kissed once more in the darkness, then climbed down from the scoreboard. When they reached the edge of the crowd, which was beginning to disperse, they went their separate ways. Dustin walked to find his parents in a daze, thinking about how perfect the day had been.

# Lane

The fireworks were exploding over his head, showering down a rainbow of colors. Lane looked at Wendy. She was completely captivated by them. She looked so beautiful and pure and made for every moment that she lived. He loved her for that. He leaned over and kissed her, something he didn't like to do in public. But how often to do you get to kiss a beautiful woman while fireworks burst above you?

Wendy kissed him back, her tongue gliding along with his. He wished they were alone and the fireworks and the night only belonged to them. But they were in a large crowd, sitting beside Daryl and Melissa. So he pulled back and let her watch the fireworks.

Dustin was nowhere to be found. Probably somewhere devouring another funnel cake, all by himself. Lane laid flat on his back and stared up at the sky, bursting with color. Wendy put a hand on his chest. She leaned over and kissed him.

In moments like these Lane thought he might be able to escape the demons, the dreams, the loneliness and guilt. There was no need for alcohol or cigarettes or anything. Wendy was able to quiet the noise in his mind, the roars of the devils who had invaded his life long ago.

Lane wanted to grab her and hold on to her as tight as he could. He decided then the only thing he would do with his life is love Wendy. He would make her happy, be there for her. Every minute of his life, every breath he took would be devoted to her. She was the only one who could save him.

# Victor

Victor stood on a bank above the inlet of the creek where he had dumped the old man's body. The key had been on the old man's neck. Yes. But Victor had thought nothing of it at the time. Just another silly trinket the old man was keeping, along with thousands of other useless trash he kept.

The key was gone now. He looked down on what was left of the old man's body. Wild animals had torn it apart, scattered the pieces all around. That had been the idea, when Victor dumped him here. Let the evidence be torn apart, ingested and digested, scattered to the corners of the Earth. Out here in this wilderness, this lonely forest where no one lived.

But now there was a truck at the trailer, and the boy had come walking out of the woods. The boy didn't live in the trailer. Victor had watched him go to the house up the hill, farther away from the woods. So that meant there were at least two people poking around much too close to the old man's body, much too soon. In a

164

few months it wouldn't matter if someone found a piece of him. Like a finger. But right now, you could still recognize his face, grotesque as it was.

Victor had climbed down into the inlet and searched around for the key. But it was dark, and all he dared use was a small flashlight. Most of the county was at the park in Crow Valley watching the fireworks, but Victor didn't want to take a chance. He knew before he arrived it was an exercise in futility. What were the odds of finding a small brass key in the middle of the night? An animal had probably swallowed it whole, anyway.

The key didn't matter too much. It just meant Victor would have to wait a little longer. Wait and be patient. Waiting, waiting, always waiting. He could figure out some way into the safe without the key. He had always been industrious and clever.

No, the problem now was the boy. Victor had seen the boy's footprints near the old man's body. He wasn't sure if the boy had seen the old man, but if he kept running around those woods, he would eventually discover it. Victor had to talk to the boy and find out if he had seen the body. Maybe scare him out of the woods somehow. Make up a ghost story so the boy wouldn't set foot among those trees ever again.

Victor took one more look at the pieces of the old man's body, sniffed the scent of decay and death, then turned and left.

# Wendy

Lane drove her home after the fireworks were over, but Wendy didn't want the night to end. She felt like there were explosions in her chest and she couldn't imagine getting into her bed alone again.

"Do you want to see my room?" Wendy asked. They were sitting in Lane's truck, holding hands. The yellow porch light put a glow on their faces.

"Yes."

"And that's not an invitation for anything else but to see my room."

"Loud and clear."

They went inside quietly, careful not to wake Granny. Wendy took him by the hand and led him into her bedroom. He stood in the center and looked around, taking it all in. She felt this weird, childish embarrassment and hoped he didn't see anything he thought was strange.

Lane walked over to her bookshelf, which took up a whole wall of her room. Wendy sat down on the bed and watched him look over the books. Every now and then he would pick one up and read the back. After a few minutes, he sat down beside her on the bed. They faced the bookshelf.

"You own a lot of books," Lane said.

"I like to read."

Lane looked around the room again. "So this is your room."

"Yeah."

"I was expecting more, I guess."

"Like what?"

"I don't know," Lane said. "Just more than a bed, a bookshelf, and a desk."

"Why?"

"You kind of built it up as something more."

"Nope," Wendy said. "I just like my privacy, that's all."

Lane chuckled and shook his head. He put a hand on her bare thigh and squeezed softly. The sensation of their skin meeting sent electricity coursing through her body. She liked it. Too much.

"Why did you invite me in?" Lane asked.

Wendy smiled and removed his hand. "Not for that."

"Then why?"

"I've only been with one man," Wendy said.

"What?"

"I've only been with my ex-husband." Wendy kept her eyes on the ground. "Like that. And even then I waited until we were married. Okay?"

Lane sighed and crossed his arms. "You think that's why I'm here?"

"No."

"Good."

Wendy looked at him. "Why are you here?"

"Because I like you."

"I mean in Crow Valley," Wendy said. "Why are you here?"

"Does that matter?" Lane asked.

"Yes. You're just living here, and you don't have a job. And you drink a lot. And I like you. So I think I deserve to know what I'm getting into before I fall for you too much more."

"I drink less since I met you."

"Give me something," Wendy said. "I have to know."

"Know what?"

"If we're bigger than whatever you're trying to drown with the whiskey."

Lane said nothing. Wendy put her head on his shoulder and rubbed his back. He was so tall and muscular, but right now he seemed so small. She wanted to lay down in bed with him and hold him until he felt strong again, until he was bigger than his pain.

"Lane."

He said nothing.

"Please."

"I had something," Lane said. "And now it's gone, and if I don't have the whiskey I can feel it. I can actually feel pain in my body, like someone took pieces of my bones out from me."

"What happened?"

Lane shook his head. "When you split up with your husband, was it like that?"

Wendy lifted her head and looked at him. She thought he might be close to tears, but his eyes weren't glassy or red. He was waiting, though, for her answer.

"Yes," she answered. "It felt like someone stuck a knife into me and twisted until I couldn't possibly hurt anymore. But I healed. I did. Slowly, but I healed."

Lane nodded and put his arm around her.

"It still hurts, though," Wendy said. "Just because you heal doesn't mean people don't leave scars."

# Daryl

Melissa took the news better than Daryl anticipated. She was angry, he could tell. But she was holding it together, listening to him as he laid out his plans. In a couple weeks, after he got paid, he would put down a deposit on an apartment and sign a lease. He'd still pay the bills for their house, too, so she wouldn't have to worry about that.

"So what, should I get a lawyer?" Melissa asked.

"It's not like that, Melissa," Daryl answered. "I just need some time. I need to figure out how to be happy on my own."

"Are you leaving me or not?"

"I need to be on my own," Daryl said. "If you're willing, I'm up for going to marriage counseling. But it has to be like this."

"I don't know what to say."

"I'm only signing a six month lease. We'll see where we are then."

Melissa sat down at the table and put her head in her hands.

169

She massaged her temples like she had a headache. Daryl didn't say anything. He wasn't here to argue or convince Melissa this was a good idea. He was moving forward with his plans.

"This is for Dustin, too," Daryl said. "I don't like coming home and feeling frustrated, angry, all that. This way, when we're together, he'll have my full attention. And I'll feel good, so our time together will be good."

Melissa looked up at him and rolled her eyes. He felt a flash of anger but he stifled it. He wasn't here to fight. She could think whatever she wanted to. This was the way it was going to be. He knew his heart and his feelings better than Melissa.

She stood up. "I'm going for a walk."

"So you understand what my plans are?" Daryl asked.

"That's why I'm going on a walk, Daryl. To see if I can wrap my brain around what you just said."

"Fine."

Daryl stood there in the kitchen and watched her go. He felt like a pressure valve in his chest had been released. It'd be even better when he was on his own, not worrying about upsetting someone. He went out to his shed to organize it. He'd probably be spending a lot of time there in the next couple weeks.

# Melissa

"He says he's leaving, but it might be only temporary," Melissa said into the phone. She cradled the receiver against her shoulder as she listened to Sherry spout off generic encouragement and advice. The woman didn't understand that Melissa didn't want a game plan or a prescription. She just wanted someone to feel sorry for her and hate Daryl as much as she did.

"For I have plans for you, to prosper and grow you," Sherry said enthusiastically. "It's right there in the Bible. A promise from God to you. I know it seems bad right now, but sometimes it's darkest before dawn."

"I know."

"Just remember, God won't put you through anything you can't handle. That's in the Bible, too, hon. Just remember to lean on his promises."

"Yes."

It went on and on like that for a while, until Melissa was exhausted. The God Sherry described seemed relentless and crammed full of sunshine. That God would have nothing to do with someone like Melissa. Someone who gave up a hundred times a day and lost sight of eternity because of everyday problems. Someone who wasn't goal-oriented. No, the God Sherry worshiped would have no time for Melissa, and she had no desire for him to exist.

"I'm just tired," Melissa said. "Isn't life hard enough already? Money problems, health problems, people dying. Shouldn't being married to someone be the easy part? Why is it so hard for him to just be with me?"

"I know it's hard, hon, but you just have to have faith." Sherry practically smiled through the phone. "Just hold on to the dream of your marriage. Cry out to God and demand blessings on your marriage. They're right there for you to claim, but you've gotta have the courage to claim them."

"Okay." Melissa tried to stop herself but she couldn't. Tears fell, and she whimpered.

"I know hon, it's tough. But God needs tough women. And I know you can be that, okay?"

Melissa nodded through her sobs.

"Now I'll be praying for you," Sherry said. "And I'll check in, okay? You call me if you need anything."

"Thanks, Sherry. Bye."

Melissa let the phone fall to the porch. She got up and went inside, straight to her bedroom. She shut off the lights and got in bed, where she cried and cried until she fell asleep.

# Dustin

Something bad had happened. Dustin knew that. His parents hadn't said anything, but both of them moved like ghosts through the house. It was like they were floating around, doing what they were supposed to do but without any life. It worried him, but he wasn't scared. Not a lot scared him anymore, not after looking into the face of the panther twice. Just the other night, there had been a noise outside his window, what sounded like footsteps. In the past it would have sent him running to his parents' room. Now he just rolled over and ignored it.

But he felt a shadow creeping over his home now, and he couldn't figure out how to make it go away. Something was wrong, and not just with his parents. He felt like storm clouds were hovering over the whole county, which was stupid. It hadn't rained in so long. Even now he tasted dust in his mouth. But it was the only thing he could compare it to. Something large and dark and insidious climbing over the hillside to destroy his family.

That was why Dustin was in his parents' room. His mom was walking, and his dad was in the shed. Dustin opened the drawer on the night stand by his dad's side of the bed. He knew in the back of it was a gun. A small .22 pistol. Dustin didn't know a lot about guns, but he knew the pistol was enough for protection in close range. And he knew how to shoot it. His dad had taught him.

He pictured the panther in his mind. The yellow eyes, the powerful jaw, the muscled shoulders. But that wasn't what scared him. Dustin had seen the panther twice, but that wasn't enough. Both times the panther had found him. He wanted to find the panther, to be the hunter for once. The shadow he felt wasn't being cast by the panther. It was something else.

Dustin grabbed the gun and the clip beside it. He check the clip to make sure it was full. He grazed his thumb against the brass shell and the lead bullet. It felt sharp and sleek. Dustin put the gun into one pocket and the clip in the other. He walked out of the room casually, in case someone had come inside. Once he was in his room, he put the clip in the gun, something his dad had always taught him not to do. Any gun in the house was supposed to be unloaded. But he had stolen the gun, which was probably worse anyway.

He put the loaded gun in his backpack, along with the peanut butter sandwich and juice box he had already packed. He put the backpack on his shoulders and left out the back door. It didn't matter. His parents didn't take much notice of the living lately. Dustin hoped Lane would be at home and not at Wendy's. He needed to see Lane badly.

# Lane

The boy looked upset, so Lane agreed to go to the woods with him. He'd been going out with Dustin, looking around for the panther. Mostly it was for exercise, a reason to get out of the trailer. Today he really wasn't in the mood, but if he stayed at the trailer, all he was going do was drink. So he threw on some boots and followed Dustin into the pine trees. He had to walk fast to keep up with the boy.

"I saw him again," Dustin said. He was walking ahead of Lane, in a hurry for some reason.

"Saw who?"

"The panther."

"So you found him?"

"He found me," Dustin said.

"You're here, so I guess you survived."

Dustin stopped and turned to Lane. "He just looked at me. For a long time. Then he left."

"Huh."

"I'm gonna show you where I saw him."

"Okay."

They followed the creek east, so far that Lane started wondering if they were still on his property. The trees began thinning and some small hills developed out of nowhere. Dustin took him to the top of a small one that overlooked the creek. Lane could see it snaking below them and then disappear into some more woods east of where they stood.

"Over there." Dustin pointed to a portion of the creek that jutted out. "I fell down the bank because I saw a deer leg lying by the creek. Landed in a blackberry bush. It's how I got these scratches."

Dustin showed Lane his arms. There were crusty scabs all over his forearms and neck. The boy seemed proud.

"Then what?" Lane asked.

"I looked up and there he was," Dustin replied. "Standing up on the top of the bank. Looking down on me."

"What'd he do?"

"Nothing. Just stared at me for a while, then left."

"Huh."

They stood and stared down. Lane was actually hoping to see the panther now. Just out of curiosity, but still. Maybe get a picture of it. Not a lot of people get a chance to see them in the wild.

"You believe me, right?" Dustin asked.

Lane looked at him. "Course I do. Why you asking?"

"No one else does."

"In my experience, little kids and animals are usually more honest than adults," Lane said. "I tend to listen to them more."

"Oh."

Lane put his hands in his pockets and sighed. It was good to be in the woods. To be sober and breathing fresh air. Wendy would like this view. He suddenly wanted to see her, to hold her and tell her a story that would make her laugh. One day he might dream of only her, instead of fire and demons and blood.

"Come see where the leg was," Dustin said.

"You go ahead. I wanna enjoy the view a little more."

"Okay. But hurry."

Dustin ran to the bank and started climbing down. Soon Lane couldn't see him anymore. He took one more look around, tried to memorize the beautiful view so he could see it in his mind before he went to sleep. He tried to put as much beauty into his brain as possible, to fight the horror he saw at night. After one more sigh of contentment, he followed after Dustin.

When he reached the bank, he heard Dustin yelp in surprise. That was the only way to describe the sound the boy made. It sent a surge of adrenaline through Lane's body. He looked down the bank to try and figure out the best way down.

"Dustin! You alright?" he called out.

"Uh...yeah." Dustin's voice was soft and fearful.

"I'm coming down."

"Nah, I'm coming up," Dustin replied. "Leg's gone."

"Hold on." Lane put his right foot on the steep grade of the bank and instantly felt it slip on the thick carpet of leaves and pine needles. He leaned his weight back to try to balance, but the foot kept sliding forward, until it caught on a root sticking out of the ground, causing his ankle to roll forward. A jolt of pain shot up through his leg and instantly made him nauseated.

Lane fell backward and then slid down a few feet on the bank before coming to a stop. His ankle throbbed and felt tight against his boot. Grunting, he used his hands and good leg to push himself up the bank until he was on level ground. He heard Dustin climbing up the bank.

"Dustin! Come help me out!" he yelled.

The boy appeared a few minutes later. His face was pale and he seemed to be shaking. Lane's ankle hurt, but he felt sorry for the kid.

"Don't worry," Lane said. "It's just sprained. I think."

"What happened?"

"Slipped and caught my foot on a root."

Dustin knelt beside him on the ground. "Can you walk?"

"Gonna have to. If you go get help, I'll be lying here after dark. Don't care to do that."

"Does it hurt a lot?" Dustin asked.

"Yeah, it does. A lot."

"What're we gonna do?"

Lane sat himself up and looked down at his ankle, thinking. "Go find me a big branch. Like a walking stick. Something I can lean on. Between that and your help, I can probably make it."

"Okay."

Dustin disappeared into the woods. Lane regretted sending him out almost instantly. Dustin had seen the panther right where they were. Maybe it was still around. Lane couldn't think clearly, not with the pain coursing up his leg. It felt like someone had sawed of his foot at the ankle.

After a few minutes, Dustin came back with a branch about five feet long. It looked like a pine of some sort. He helped Lane stand up onto his left foot, then handed him the branch. Lane took it and leaned some weight on it. It felt solid and was fairly straight.

"I think this'll do," he said.

They slowly made their way back to Lane's trailer. It took them twice as long as it did to get to the hills by the creek. Lane had to stop and rest more than a couple times. He was sorry that he ruined Dustin's day, and told the boy as much once they were inside the trailer and he was resting on his recliner.

"Don't worry about it." Dustin sat on the floor in front of him. "It was an accident."

"Still."

Dustin sipped on a soda that he'd gotten out of the fridge. There was a smudge of dirt on his face. Sometimes Lane wished he was a boy again. Dustin fiddled with the tab on the can.

"What'd you see down there?" Lane asked.

"What?"

"You yelled. Right before I sprained my ankle. What made you yell?"

"Oh." Dustin took a long gulp of the soda. "Nothing. I

178

thought I saw a snake, but it was just a vine."

"Huh." Lane looked at Dustin. He was no body language expert, but the boy was definitely lying. It was probably nothing, though, and there wasn't much Lane could do about it anyway. He couldn't go back and look. Not in his condition.

"What're you gonna do?" Dustin asked.

"I'm gonna call Wendy and hope she feels sorry me."

# Victor

Shelley's Diner was for truck drivers and drunks and people struggling with obesity. Victor was none of those things, so he'd never been in the restaurant. If you could even call it a restaurant. More like a grease shack that served food. Just being in the parking lot disgusted him.

But not as much as the man he was watching. The forest ranger or game warden. Whatever he was. This grown man, married with at least one child, was panting after the tall, blonde waitress in Shelley's. Like he was a teenager. Disgusting. Victor had been watching him through the window for more than an hour.

Victor rolled his eyes and went into Shelley's.

The place smelled as filthy as it looked. Victor choked back a gag and steadied himself. He was going to have to order some food from this wretched kitchen. He sat down near the game warden, leaving a stool between them. The blonde waitress came over, Trisha was her name according to the plastic badge she wore, and took his order. She came back with a diet soda a minute later. Victor sipped it.

He turned to the game warden. "Good evening."

"Evening."

"Did you get the burger?"

"I did."

"I love the burgers here," Victor said. He'd never had a hamburger from Shelley's.

"Yeah, they're pretty good."

"Not as good as the staff, though." Victor nodded toward Trisha, who was giving food to a party at a booth across the diner. The game warden flashed an uncomfortable smile and nodded, then looked down at the drink he was holding. Victor wanted to laugh. Okay to gawk at the long-legged blonde as long as you don't talk about it.

"Of course, I come for the conversation more than anything else," Victor said.

"That so."

"Yes. I like to talk to strangers, find out their stories, hear what motivates them, what makes them tick."

"You some sort of reporter?"

"No. Just...interested in others. My name is Victor."

"Daryl."

Victor extended his thin hand. Daryl thought for a moment and then reached out and shook it. His hand was meaty and strong. He could crush Victor's hand if he wanted to.

"So, Daryl, what do you do?" Victor asked. He loved asking questions he already had the answer to.

"I'm the game warden for Crow County."

Game warden, not forest ranger. "That sounds interesting."

"It can be, at times. What about you?"

"Handyman. I mow yards, build flowerbeds, odd jobs," Victor replied. "Things like that."

"Huh. You get a lot of work?"

"Yes."

Trisha brought the hamburger over and set it in front of him.

181

Victor thanked her and then took a giant bite of the burger, pretending to enjoy it. He had to concentrate to swallow it. When it finally went down, he sighed in mock pleasure.

"Good stuff."

"Yup," Daryl muttered.

"My son always loved the hamburgers from here," Victor said. He had no children.

"Yeah?"

"We would come here after his baseball games when he was young." Victor sipped his soda. "He's grown now, moved across the country."

"You get to see him much?" Daryl asked.

"A little. Around the holidays, and usually I take a trip to see him in the summer."

"Where's he living?"

"California. Near the Oregon border."

"Oh."

"Do you have any children?" Victor asked.

"Yeah, a son. He's twelve, be thirteen in the fall."

"Boys are the best," Victor said. "Easy to entertain."

"Yeah, my boy plays baseball, too. Pretty good at it, too."

"Good, good." Victor looked over at Daryl, made eye contact. Watched the large man squirm. It made him want to laugh. He loved making men bigger than him uncomfortable, all with a few words.

Victor thought about the razor blade in his pocket and what he could do to Daryl if he wanted. If given the opportunity.

"Well, Victor, it was good talking to you," Daryl said. He stood up and wiped his face with a napkin.

"I feel the same. Have a good evening."

Victor watched Daryl pay at the register. He and Trisha talked for a few more minutes, laughing and flirting. Touching one another. Victor pretended to eat the hamburger some more. He'd been watching the game warden and his family from a distance for a few days. Now he had been close.

182

Victor couldn't tell if the boy had seen the body. Or rather, what was left of the body. He would have said something by now, especially to his father. Surely. Maybe he would talk to the boy. That would help. Victor would be able to see how the boy talked, how he reacted to questions. Maybe he had seen the body. Maybe not. Victor would have to wait to find out. Always waiting.

# Wendy

Lane was laid up in his recliner, his swollen ankle propped up with a pillow. Wendy put her hands on her hips and looked down on him with pity. It was obviously painful. He might have needed to go to the hospital. But she knew he wasn't going to go for that.

"I feel bad for you," Wendy said. "I do."

"Then why're you smiling?" Lane asked.

"Well, it's kinda funny." Wendy knelt beside him and ran her fingers through his hair. "And you look cute like this."

"I didn't ask you to come over and gawk at me."

"I know, but it's a perk of the job, my dear."

Wendy stood up and looked over the trailer. It was filthy. Cans of beer lying around, empty bottles of whiskey. Fast food bags here and there. A thick layer of dust on everything. The man had only been here a few months but he'd sure made a mess of the place.

"You'd think you would have tidied up the place a bit before

184

you invited me over," Wendy said, raising her eyebrows and smirking.

"Ha. What do people say? My housekeeper is on vacation?"

"I think your housekeeper never showed up for the job."

"Funny."

"I know I offered to come over here and cook for you, but I've got to clean before I can cook anything," Wendy said. "I can't imagine preparing a meal without sterilizing your kitchen."

Lane shrugged. "Have at it."

Wendy loaded up the dishwasher with every dish clogging the sink and then started scrubbing the counters. After that, she swept the small kitchen floor and then cleaned the stove. When she was satisfied with the condition of the kitchen, she made a quick casserole with canned chicken, cheese, and rice and put it in the oven.

While the casserole baked, she started walking around, picking up the clothes that had been thrown around the room. Shirts, jeans, and socks were laying everywhere. She shook her head and wondered what she had gotten into.

"I hope you have a washing machine," she said to Lane, laundry basket on her hip.

"Down the hall, second door on your left."

Wendy went through the kitchen and down the narrow hallway. She passed the first door, which was open and revealed a tiny room with a desk and a twin bed. It was decorated nicely and was fairly clean. She shook her head again and thought it was such a shame that Lane was wrecking what had once been a nice little home.

The second door was a bathroom that had a washer and dryer crammed inside. There wasn't very much room to maneuver, but Wendy was fairly petite and could get around. She started the washer and poured in some detergent, then started tossing clothes inside. When she grabbed a pair of jeans, she would go through all the pockets to make sure there was nothing inside, like pens or money or anything else that would make a mess in the washer.

As she was going through the last pair of jeans, she felt something cold and metal in the front right pocket. She pulled it out and found a gold wedding band. It was dull and dirty and obviously a man's. Obviously Lane's. Wendy let the jeans fall into the washer as she held the ring in her hand, staring at it. A thousand questions went through her mind, enough to drown her in a sea of anxiety. But Wendy was pragmatic and calm and knew that if she wanted answers, Lane was sitting in the living room.

She sat down beside him and crossed her legs. He must have known something was wrong by the look on her face. She handed him the ring.

"Are you still hung up on her?" Wendy asked.

Lane held the ring between his thumb and index finger. "Yes."

"Is that why you drink?"

He nodded.

"You still love her?"

"Yeah."

She tried to fight it, but the tears came to her eyes anyway. "I think I should go then. I don't want to waste my time or yours."

Wendy stood to go. Lane's hand reached out quickly and grabbed her arm. His grip was strong and hurt her wrist. She tried to pull away but he held tightly.

"Wendy…" Lane's voice cracked.

"Quit!" Wendy shook her arm again but he held firm.

"She's gone."

Wendy glared down at Lane and saw tears flowing down his cheeks. She started crying too, like the sight of his tears gave her heart permission to let go.

"She died a little more than a year ago," Lane said. "Her and my son."

Wendy's arm fell limp and Lane let go of her wrist. The tears kept coming down his cheeks, but he didn't make any sound. Just sat there while his eyeballs leaked like a shoddy dam. There were a thousand things Wendy wanted to ask and say and do, but none of them seemed right. So she just knelt beside him and held his hand for a long time.

When the tears stopped, she asked, "What happened?"

"A car wreck," Lane said. "A drunk driver. He drifted into the other lane, hit'em head on. All three of them died. There. Out there on the road."

He started crying again.

Wendy slowly crawled into the recliner with him, careful not to touch his ankle. She wrapped her arms around as much of him as she could and buried her face in his neck. They laid there for holding each other, crying with each other. Wendy decided then that all the pieces of her broken heart belonged to Lane Carter.

# Daryl

The truck wasn't as full as Daryl thought it would be. He didn't have many belongings. And he wanted to leave most of the furniture for Melissa and Dustin. His apartment was going to be sparse for a while. The only thing he'd bought was a full mattress and a bed frame. So moving wasn't hard.

Melissa was gone, probably with Sherry, the pastor's wife. Funny, Daryl thought that the pastor would've come around and tried to talk him out of this move. But he didn't. No one from the church did. Of course, he and Melissa hadn't broadcast their problems, like some couples did. Maybe no one knew.

Dustin was gone, too. Melissa had arranged for him to go over to a friend's house for the afternoon. It'd gone better than expected when they told the boy. Daryl thought he would cry and break down, but Dustin just nodded. It kind of worried Daryl. He walked back in the house and stuck his head in the boy's room. He looked over it for a while and felt sad. But it was for the best. He would be no good to Dustin if he was angry and sad all the time. No kind of father, nothing worth looking up to. His son needed a real man to model his life after. Not some barely alive ghost drifting through life on cruise control.

Daryl drove to the apartment, which took about thirty minutes. A good distance. Close, but far enough away to have some space. To have some distance and relief. He carried all the boxes inside and shut the door. He turned the thermostat down until the air was nice and chilly. The heat was becoming terrible. He sat down on the bed and realized he didn't have sheets. It looked like he was going to Wal-Mart.

The apartment was quiet and at first Daryl liked it. But then he missed the noise of other people, even though Melissa and Dustin were never loud. Just the noise of dishes being washed, footsteps on floors. It was gone, replaced by silence and the hum of the air conditioning. He got up and started unpacking.

# Melissa

Things were missing, were out of place. Like her home had been robbed. In a sense, it had. Daryl's things were gone, plucked out of the mosaic of their house like pieces from a jigsaw puzzle. It made her sad, and she started crying not long after walking into the house.

She'd arranged for Dustin to spend the night at his friend's house. Dustin and Curtis got along well, she thought. She hoped they had a good time together, and that Dustin would forget about the missing pieces of his home for a few hours.

Melissa went to the bedroom and opened her sock drawer. She reached to the back and pulled out the bottle of whiskey she'd taken from Lane. It was heavy, and the glass felt cool. She opened it, took a long drink, and as it burned her throat, felt like she was going to vomit. She sat down on the bed and gathered herself, taking one sip and then another until it didn't burn as much.

She started to get sleepy but it felt good. Tears were coming down her face and she thought that was odd, because it didn't feel like she was crying at all. She felt like she was falling down a dark hole, and it was nice. There was nothing in the hole. No pain, no shame or embarrassment or failure or hurt. She drank more so she could fall deeper down.

# Lane

To say he was sleeping soundly would be a lie, but Lane had dozed off. And there weren't any dreams, which was rare. So when he heard the loud knocking on his door and startled awake, he became angry. He jumped out of bed and stomped to the front door. The knocking hadn't stopped. Someone was pounding on the door like a maniac. Lane flung the door open, fists clenched.

Standing in front of him, though, was Melissa. And she was drunk. Her eyes were swollen and bloodshot, her cheeks flush. Her hair was wild, and she rocked side to side as she stood on his back porch. She was wearing a light blue robe that was loosely tied at the waist. She was holding at empty bottle of whiskey. At first, it seemed like she didn't even notice he'd answered the door. Just stared through him like he wasn't there.

"Melissa?"

Speaking her name broke her trance. She blinked a few times

and then held up the bottle close to his face. Lane took a step back.

"I need some more," Melissa said. "Please."

She let the bottle fall to the porch. It clanged loudly and rolled across the wood boards. Melissa took a step back from the door and looked like she was about to collapse. Lane was too stunned to do anything.

"Are you alright?" he asked. "Do you need help?"

"Daryl moved out today."

Melissa tried to take a step forward, but her foot caught an uneven board and she pitched forward. Lane stepped out of the door and caught her, wrapping her in his arms to steady her. Their faces were close and her breath smelled so much like whiskey it burnt his nose. Lane moved around so that he was beside her and brought her into the trailer. He helped her onto the couch and then sat beside her.

"You've had too much to drink," he said.

"I know."

"Where's Dustin? Is he alone at the house?"

"No. At a friend's house."

Melissa laid back into the couch and moaned. She was probably feeling sick to her stomach. Lane wondered if he should take her to a hospital or just back to her house. There was a lot of whiskey left in the bottle he gave her. But she would probably be okay. Just feel like a wreck in the morning.

"Sit tight," Lane said. "I'm going to get you some water."

He went to the kitchen and poured a tall glass of water and added ice. The clock on the microwave told him it was well after two in the morning. He sighed and headed back to the living room. When he opened the door, he found Melissa standing by the couch. Her robe was on the floor in front of her.

She was wearing some sort of lingerie. It was purple, and Lane could see through most of it. It was low cut, exposing most of the tops of her breasts, and stopped just a few inches after her hips. She had one hand on her hip and turned slightly, like she was modeling. But she couldn't stay very steady.

"Do you like this?" she asked.

"Melissa."

"I wore it on my honey moon," she said. "Years ago. Still fits."

"Put your robe back on."

"Do you want to make love to me?" Melissa asked. "Make love to me, Lane."

"You're drunk. And married."

"I'm only one of those." Melissa used a finger to slide one of the straps off of her shoulder. "Daryl doesn't own me and doesn't care what I do anymore. He's gone. And you're here. Come kiss me."

Lane looked into her eyes. "This isn't happening."

"Let's go to the bedroom." Melissa took a step and then stopped. Her head jerked for a second and she bent over. Lane closed his eyes as she vomited onto her robe and the floor. He listened to her wretch and gag for a few minutes. He opened his eyes. She had crumpled to the floor and was sobbing.

Lane picked her up and laid her on the couch, careful to put her on her side in case she vomited again. He got a wash cloth and wiped off her mouth, then helped her sip some of the water. He cleaned up the floor while Melissa sipped the water.

"I'm sorry," she murmured. "So sorry."

"It's okay." Lane scrubbed the carpet and then found some cinnamon air freshener in an aerosol can. Melissa's eyes slowly closed and she fell asleep. Lane found a sheet and put it over her. He stood over her for a few moments, studying her. She looked horrible. He glanced at the clock. It was after three now.

He thought about calling Wendy and asking her what to do. But it was so late, and he didn't want to wake her up. He decided to call her early in the morning. It wasn't like he was going back to sleep now. Lane turned off all the lights and went back to the bedroom, where he stared up at the ceiling and tried to ignore the smell of vomit wafting in from the living room. And then, somehow, he fell asleep and didn't dream.

# Dustin

The house was empty. Dustin had been through every room and walked around the outside. No one. He knew his dad would be gone. But his mother was missing, too. Her car was parked by the house, though. Curtis's mom had dropped Dustin off about an hour ago. Now he just sat on the floor in his bedroom.

He'd been alone before, so he wasn't really scared of that. This was something different. A feeling he couldn't shake, a feeling he would call dread if someone forced him to label it. The shadow that had been hanging over his family for so long had grown darker, like a powerful thunderstorm was about to let loose with all its fury.

His father was gone, and Dustin didn't know when he would see him again. His father had said something about the next weekend, but Dustin didn't really care about that. It wasn't like a friend had left his house and the next weekend would be when they were hanging out. A presence was gone. He didn't feel safe anymore, not even in his own house. His mother cared for him, Dustin knew that. But she wasn't his dad.

He waited another fifteen or twenty minutes. His mom didn't show up, and he'd long given up on his dad showing up anywhere. Dustin choked back a panicked sob and grabbed his backpack. He ran down to the woods as fast as he could. When he passed Lane's trailer, he noticed Wendy standing on the porch, knocking on the door. Dustin rolled his eyes and ran faster, until he was deep in the woods, surrounded by the darkness of ancient pines.

# Wendy

Usually Lane was on the back porch this late in the morning. The man really didn't sleep. Not that Wendy could blame him. Not after what she knew now. He'd called her early this morning, but she was in the shower. She'd tried calling him back, but the call didn't go through. The phone service this far out from town was hit or miss sometimes.

She knocked on the door and waited. She heard shuffling inside. Lane was probably still limping from his ankle sprain. It'd been pretty bad. She was glad he had called, because she had been thinking about coming over and making him breakfast. It would be fun, to sit around, eat together on the porch while the day heated up. Maybe they'd see some deer.

Lane opened the door and blocked the frame with his whole body. He looked tired. But still handsome. He leaned down and kissed her.

"Morning," he said. "What're you doing here?"

"I saw you called," Wendy replied. "I tried calling you back, but there was no answer. So I just came over. Thought we could have breakfast."

"Wendy, I called you for a reason."

Wendy held up the pancake mix she was holding. "We can make pancakes."

"Something happened last night."

Wendy felt her heart drop into her belly. "Okay. What?"

Lane moved to the side so she could see into the trailer. On the couch behind him was Melissa. She was half-covered by a sheet and wearing some sort of night gown. Now Wendy's heart started beating fast. Calm down, she told herself. He's going to tell you what's going on.

"What's this?" she asked.

"She showed up last night around two in the morning, drunk. I guess her and Daryl split up, and she's not taking it well. She asked me to sleep with her and then threw up on my floor. After that she fell asleep on the couch. That's why I called you so early this morning."

Wendy stared at him, trying to picture the situation in her mind.

"Nothing happened, Wendy. I promise. I know it looks bad, but nothing happened."

She reached out and took his hand. "I believe you. I know nothing happened."

Lane looked relieved. He stepped back and motioned for her to come inside. For a while the two of them just stood over Melissa and watched her sleep. Wendy felt sad for her. She could tell Lane felt very nervous and was waiting for her to do something.

"Why don't you get in the shower," Wendy said. "Take a long shower. I'll wake her up and get her home, okay?"

Lane nodded and disappeared into the bathroom. Wendy put her things on the kitchen table and went back to couch. She squatted down so that she was eye level with Melissa. She took Melissa's hand and squeezed it gently a few times. After a moment, Melissa's eyes opened. She looked around wildly like she didn't know where she was.

"Melissa, it's me. Wendy."

Melissa squinted her eyes and frowned deeply, putting creases in her forehead. "Wendy?"

"Yeah, it's me. From church."

"Yeah." Melissa moaned softly and looked around. "Am I at Lane's?"

Wendy nodded.

"Oh, God. Oh, God. I thought it was a dream."

"It wasn't," Wendy said.

"Oh God, Wendy. Nothing happened. I was acting crazy." Melissa started to cry. "Daryl left. And I drank a lot. I wasn't myself. You have to know that. I wasn't myself. I wasn't thinking. I was drunk. That's not me."

"Shh." Wendy gently stroked Melissa's hand. "It's okay. I'm going to take you home."

Melissa nodded. She sat up and gagged. Wendy ran and got a small trash can from the unoccupied bathroom. She held Melissa's hair while she vomited into the trash can. Melissa started crying again.

"I'm sorry, Wendy."

"It's okay."

Wendy drove Melissa to her home just up the road from Lane's. She helped her out of the night gown, which was stained with vomit, into some sweat pants and a t-shirt. After giving her lots of water and a few aspirin, she put Melissa in bed. She drove back down to Lane's. He was sitting on the porch, smoking a cigarette.

"Those are gonna kill you," she said as she walked up the steps. "You should stop."

"Helps calm the nerves." Lane dropped the cigarette on the porch and ground it out with his boot. "Listen–"

"I already told you, I believe you. Let's not worry about it."

"You sure?"

"I trust you," Wendy said. "I trust you a lot."

"Thank you."

"Just don't let half-naked women sleeping on your couch become a habit," Wendy said.

Lane smiled. "Yes, ma'am."

"You want me to make those pancakes?"

Lane nodded. They went inside and had breakfast together. Afterwards, they went to Lane's bedroom and kissed for a long time on his bed. When it seemed like it was going too far, Wendy got up and asked Lane if he felt like he could walk. She thought it would be good for him to move around so his ankle didn't get to stiff.

They took a short walk around his property, at the edge of the woods. Lane told her about searching for the panther with Dustin and how he liked spending time with the boy. She liked hearing him talk about it and pictured him as a father.

Wendy wondered if Lane loved her, even though their time together had been short. She hoped he did. It seemed like it. But you never knew if someone loved you until they saw all your scars. Lane wore his out in the open. They were easy to see. Wendy kept hers hidden away. She always had.

# Victor

It took two days, but Victor got the safe open. With a combination of high powered drills and an acetylene torch, he was able to get the key lock off. He did it all during the day, too.

He had thought about coming at night, but decided that would be more suspicious. If someone came upon him during the day, he could stick to his story, the ruse that he was a dedicated employee who loved the old man so much he refused to neglect his duties, even though he was no longer getting paid.

But once the safe was open, Victor was paid in full. Ten solid gold bars gleamed in the dusty shadows of the shed. Victor picked one up and held it. Put it up to his cheek and felt the cold metal on his skin. Always waiting, waiting. Waiting for this. To see the glint of the gold, to feel how heavy it was in his hands.

The old man had been careful. Yes. But the old man couldn't control what he said in his sleep. Couldn't keep the thought of his precious gold inside his mind forever. Couldn't help but whisper about it. And Victor had been there, listening. And waiting.

Victor put the gold in a large suitcase he'd brought. He put it in the trunk of his car and started toward home. Or at least what was to be his home for a few more weeks. No more waiting, no more patience. Plans could be made. Deposits could be paid. The waiting was over.

But something still nagged at his mind. A loose end. He couldn't leave a witness, couldn't live the rest of his life looking over his shoulder. He had to know for sure that he was safe, and that meant taking care of one more thing.

The boy.

# Daryl

A few candles were lit, but not anything overtly romantic. Just enough to make the place look classy and inviting. Daryl didn't know a lot about creating ambiance, but he knew that lighting just a couple of candles could turn a shabby room into something better. And his apartment was pretty shabby at the moment.

Trisha sat across from him. They were eating supper on a flimsy card table he'd taken from his home. His former home. He'd thrown a cheap table cloth over the table so it didn't look too bad. And he hadn't cooked. Everything they were eating was from a local chicken place. Fried chicken, mashed potatoes, fried okra, and rolls. He could feel his cholesterol going up with every bite, but he didn't care. It tasted good, and this beautiful woman was sitting across from him.

Beautiful girl. Daryl was almost twice her age.

He'd bought some wine and only now, as he was pouring it, did he wonder if Trisha was over 21. Of course she was. Maybe. Daryl suddenly felt old and fat and wrinkled. He was glad the room was dark. Trisha wouldn't be able to see him blushing, aware of how ridiculous it was for him to be here with her while his wife and son were miles away.

But she was here. Eating a meal with him. That's what people did when they wanted to spend time with each other. They broke bread. She hadn't hesitated when he asked her over. Be more confident, he told himself. Be sure of yourself.

"It's a nice place," Trisha said.

"It's a little small, but it is nice."

"You don't need a lot of space. It's just you."

"That's true."

Trisha picked up a piece of okra and put it in her mouth. God, the girl could look good chomping on fried vegetables. The woman, he corrected himself. She's a woman. A grown woman who has a grown woman's body and makes adult decisions. Like him.

After they finished eating they went to the balcony and sat on two cheap plastic chairs Daryl had bought. Trisha produced a pack of cigarettes from her purse and lit one. Daryl watched the smoke curl up into the air.

"I didn't know you smoked," he said.

"I don't always. But sometimes it feels right."

She offered the pack to him and he took one. He hadn't smoked in more than a decade. Longer than that. He put the cigarette into the flame of Trisha's lighter and watched it catch fire. He inhaled and felt the smoke drift into his lungs. It didn't make him cough, which surprised him.

"I like that you're at the back of the complex," Trisha said. His balcony looked out over a field that stretched for almost a mile before it ended at narrow road. "It's peaceful."

"Yeah, I like it," Daryl said. "Quiet."

They sat there smoking and talking for about an hour. Daryl felt strange the whole time and couldn't place why. Maybe it was just being alone with a woman who wasn't Melissa. He wondered if that feeling would ever go away.

He didn't know how to end the evening. Was Trisha waiting on him to say something? To kiss her? Or maybe she didn't think of him that way. He didn't know if he could make a move on a woman anymore, didn't really even remember how. So he just kept conversation moving and watched her, waiting for some sign of what to do.

But luckily Trisha solved the problem for him and left easily. She hugged him before she left, though. Not a friendly hug, either. She leaned her whole body in and stayed with him for a few long seconds. Daryl wrapped his arms around her skinny waist and breathed in her peculiar scent, the mixture of perfume and smoke. It felt good to hold her, even briefly.

After she was gone, Daryl turned out all the lights and turned on the radio beside his bed. The first couple of nights had been deathly quiet, and it had been hard to sleep. So he tuned in some country station and put the volume low. He laid on his back and stared at the dark ceiling while some old familiar country song played. It was a song he knew, but he couldn't place it in his mind. He hummed a few bars and then slowly fell asleep.

# Melissa

The bath water was lukewarm. Melissa sank as far as she could into it and remembered some Bible verse about a town that was neither hot nor cold. Because the town was lukewarm, God was going to vomit them out of his mouth. She didn't really understand what that meant, but it sounded horrible. It probably meant destruction.

Her marriage had been lukewarm and now God had vomited it out. Or maybe Daryl had. Either way, it was nothing now. And if her marriage was her life, then her life was nothing. Nothing.

The thought had crossed her mind before she drew the bath. How easy would it be to end her life, just as her marriage ended? There was enough medicine in the kitchen cabinet to do it. Or maybe a couple of quick slices to her wrists.

Dustin was the only reason she didn't. Dustin would be the

one to find her. No, her son would be a man by the time he buried her deep in the East Texas clay.

Melissa was able to dry herself off and get dressed before she started crying. She stood in front of the mirror and looked at herself. The image in front of her was distorted by tears. She sunk to the floor, leaned against the bed and sobbed so hard she thought her ribs might break.

# Dustin

Dustin came back home in a bad mood. It didn't get better when he found the house empty and quiet. After he went to his room and threw his backpack on the ground, he went to the bathroom and washed the sweat off his face, making sure to slam the door and throw the towel against the mirror.

When he came out of the bathroom, he heard a sound. He stood in the hall and listened. It sounded like whimpering, like a dog was crying. He followed the sound to his parents' bedroom. To his mom's bedroom. He opened the door.

His mom was on the floor crying. She was grabbing her chest like it hurt and making a weird sound. Like she was choking on her tears. She didn't even notice him standing there watching.

The anger melted away and tears started flowing out of Dustin, too. He fell into his mom's lap. She gasped as first, startled by him. But then she wrapped her arms around him and held him tight, tighter than she ever had. Her clothes were wet with tears and soon his were, too. He didn't care.

They held each other, their faces close, tears mingling together and baptizing both of them while the world fell apart outside.

# Lane

The demons came in full force this time. Not just a few, not just dozens. At least a hundred. Maybe more. Lane knew it was a dream, but there are times when dreams seem to bleed into reality and it becomes hard to distinguish between the two. So Lane laid in bed, thinking he was dreaming but also expecting to be killed by whatever these things were. He was prepared to die. Part of him wanted to die. So much of him was already dead.

But then Wendy was there, walking among the demons. She was glowing, like she was a saint or divine. Like a goddess flowing through the darkness. She wore a white robe and a crown of flowers on her head. She touched the demons on the head and they crumpled before her, defeated and destroyed.

There were too many of them, though. They overcame her, wrapped their claws around her and pulled her down into hell with them. They laughed loudly, and the sound echoed all around Lane. He screamed at them but they just smiled back, their teeth and limbs stained with blood.

"We will have her," they said in unison. "We will have her because you have brought her to us."

Lane screamed and woke up covered in sweat. His hands were shaking.

Lane rushed into the kitchen and found a bottle of whiskey. He drank it straight from the bottle, chugging it like it was water. It burned his throat and stomach and he threw up. He stared at the vomit on the floor for a moment and then drank more. He kept drinking until the bottle was empty. Then he found another.

He drank until there was no more liquor left in his trailer. And then he prayed to God for more liquor. He searched the house frantically, hoping to find a bottle he'd forgotten about. But he couldn't. Then he prayed to God for death and prayed that Wendy would forget about him forever.

Lane walked outside and looked up at the sky.

"Why am I even here?" he screamed. "Why did you leave me here to die slow? Why couldn't I go quick, like them?"

He walked into the field behind his house and fell down into the tall grass. It didn't hurt because he couldn't feel anything. He held out both middle fingers to the sky.

"I hate you!" he screamed. The he passed out.

# Victor

The gold was in two duffel bags in Victor's closet. He would be moving them soon. The moon was full and bright. There were no clouds to obscure it. It hadn't rained in so long.

Victor scratched a tilted cross onto a tree in his backyard. There were two others on the tree and they all leaned to the right.

He took the rat from the bucket beside him and snapped its neck. He held the rat while the last few nerves fired and twitched. When it was still, he took a knife and made an incision down the rat's belly. He held the rat's body up to the tree and smeared the flowing blood onto the third cross.

"God of the Underneath, give me this soul," Victor whispered. He lifted his hands to the sky, to the moon, and asked again. "God of the Underneath, give me this soul."

Victor put the bloody rat carcass in the bucket and dumped gasoline on it. He threw a match into the bucket and watched the body burn. Soon the bucket itself melted, liquid plastic running

212

everywhere. He watched it until the fire died.

Victor turned and walked back to his house. He washed his hands thoroughly and then went through his nightly ritual. The ritual that would clean him. He thought about the bloodstained cross on the tree in his yard. He remembered how the God of the Underneath had given him two souls before. Victor knew he would have another. The Great God of the Underneath had yellow eyes that watched all.

The boy would be delivered into Victor's hands.

# Daryl

The moon was full and bright. No clouds. Daryl sat in a folding chair on his balcony smoking cigarettes. He'd bought them earlier in the day. Melissa would have never let him smoke, not even outside. Not that she could stop him. It was really impossible to change a person in a relationship. You just hoped the weight of your expectations eventually broke their will. At least that's how Daryl saw it.

When the cigarette in his mouth burned low, he put it out beneath his boot and lit another. He liked smoking. But it wasn't as good alone.

That was why he was out here on the balcony, smoking away. The apartment was dark and quiet. Even the noise of the radio couldn't eliminate the silence. Out here, under the sky, he at least felt like he was a part of the world. He wondered what Melissa and Dustin were doing. He wondered if the boy hated him now.

Daryl would be going to pick him up this weekend. They'd

spend some time together and Daryl could see how Dustin was feeling. Maybe they'd play a game here at the apartment. Daryl could teach him poker. Anything to lift the cloud of quiet.

Daryl put the cigarette out and went inside. He didn't bother to turn on any lights. He fell into bed, with his clothes still on, and laid there for hours, wondering whether he'd made the right decision. At three in the morning he convinced himself that moving out made sense. It was best for everyone. Then he fell asleep.

# Dustin

The sunlight woke Dustin, and it made him angry. It was always shining. There was no break from the relentless heat. Texas summers were hot and long, but this one seemed unbearable.

It was morning, early morning, and the sheets around him felt like a hot cloth already. The air conditioner was blowing cold air but it didn't seem to help.

He got up and poured a bowl of cereal. At first he wondered where his mom was but then he heard her outside. She was doing yard work. It seemed like whenever grownups were upset they worked outside, either in the yard or in a shop. Maybe it was just his parents.

Dustin watched cartoons as he ate the cereal. He wasn't very hungry, but he knew he would get hungry later if he didn't eat something. His mom walked in a few minutes later and kissed him on the forehead.

"Mom?"

"What honey?" she replied. She was walking to the kitchen but had stopped when he called her.

"Can I have a dog?" Dustin asked.

She looked at him like she was confused. "I guess so."

"Okay. Thanks."

His mom stayed there, hands on her hips, looking at him. "Why do you want one?"

"What?"

"You've never really wanted one before," she said. "Why now?"

Dustin shrugged his shoulders. "I don't know. I just think it would be cool."

"Okay."

His mom went to the kitchen and started cleaning. She was cleaning a lot lately. Probably to take her mind off things. He understood. Their house was the cleanest he'd ever seen it. Except his room.

When he finished the cereal he grabbed his backpack and left to search the woods, with a promise to his mom to come back around noon for lunch. The second he stepped outside beads of sweat appeared on his forehead. As soon as he was out of sight of the house, Dustin ran over to a large bush beside the road. Behind it was a plastic grocery bag full of glass bottles.

He'd been collecting them for a while, ever since he took his dad's gun. Today he was going to practice shooting with the gun, and he was going to use the bottles as targets. He didn't stop at Lane's trailer, because he didn't want Lane to know that he had the gun. Dustin knew he could get in trouble for having it, but he wanted to get good at shooting it. So he hurried past Lane's trailer and didn't even look in its direction.

He walked deep into the woods, where it was dark and thick with trees. There was no way to completely muffle the sound, but maybe he could get away with shooting the gun here. Even if Lane heard the gunshots, he probably wouldn't care. The important thing was to make sure his mom didn't hear. And there was no way she would hear the gunshots where he was now.

He set up about a dozen bottles on a rotting log. They were all kinds of different bottles he'd found along the side of the road. He walked about twenty feet away and set down his backpack. He pulled out the gun and held it in his palm, looking at it. It was heavier than he remembered.

His dad had shown him how to shoot about a year ago. Dustin still remembered how, but he knew he wasn't very good. He might need to use it one day. To protect himself. Not from the panther, though. The large cat had already had two opportunities to kill him and had walked away both times. No, he just wanted in case he came upon another hog. Or maybe a bobcat. Something wild and dangerous.

Dustin put the clip into the gun and then clicked off the safety. He spread his feet and held the gun with two hands in front of him. He closed one eye and peered down the barrel at the sight. He took aim at a bottle and squeezed the trigger. The gun exploded in his hand and kicked back hard. Some smoke circled the air above him, and he heard the bullet ricochet through the woods. The bottle stood untouched.

Dustin took a breath and aimed again. He squeezed the trigger and felt the kick. This time, though, the bottle exploded. Glass flew everywhere. Dustin smiled. It felt good. He took aim at the next bottle and tried again. He shot at the bottles until the clip was empty. Then he reloaded the clip and started shooting again. He shot faster and faster each time.

He loved the way it felt and went through an entire box of bullets.

# Lane

Gunshots rang out through the heavy morning air and woke Lane. At first he thought they were a dream, another horrible dream. But he opened his eyes and still heard them. They were far away, little explosions bursting from deep in the woods. His head ached so badly that every shot shook his body with tiny tremors of pain.

He was lying on his back in the field near his trailer. His clothes were covered in a light dew and he was beginning to sweat. It was so hot. He looked up at the sky and saw nothing but blue. The sun was just coming up over the pines in the distance. He figured it to be about nine or ten o'clock.

Lane sat up and immediately felt nauseated. He rubbed his eyes and concentrated hard to keep whatever was in his stomach from reappearing. He looked over to his right at his trailer. It seemed so far away at the moment. Crawling back to it didn't sound unreasonable, but he was able to collect himself and start staggering toward it.

The dreams made him sick, even in the daylight. Lane made the decision easily. Probably even made it during the night, when he was under the haze of the whiskey. He wouldn't drag Wendy into his personal hell, wouldn't destroy her light and love with his agony.

Lane went to his bedroom and started packing.

# Wendy

Wendy smiled as she drove. She and Lane were going to eat breakfast and then run some errands. It was starting to feel like they were a real couple, something she hadn't experienced in years. They had some things to work out for sure, but it felt real to her. Safe.

When she drove up to Lane's trailer, though, she found him throwing duffel bags into his truck. He looked horrible. His eyes were bloodshot, and he looked pale and sweaty. The way he was moving, running back and forth to the truck, scared her. She jumped out of the car and ran over to him.

"What's going on?" she asked. "Are you okay?"

Lane stopped and looked down at her, almost in tears. "I have to go."

"Go? Go where? Is something wrong? Did something happen to your parents?"

"No, it's not that. It's not them. I just have to go."

Lane pushed past her and ran back into the house. Wendy stood there, stunned, staring at the truck. He was serious. She felt panic rise in her chest and wondered what she did to make him run. She ran into the house and found him in his bedroom.

"Lane, stop," she said. "Tell me what's going on."

"I have to leave, Wendy. That's it."

"Why?"

"I just do."

Wendy stood in front of him and grabbed his shirt. "Be a man and tell me why."

"I'll hurt you." Lane sniffed and turned his head. "One day. I'll hurt you somehow. You don't need me dragging you down into this mess."

"Lane, I know you've been through a lot and I know you're scared of hurting me and getting hurt again, but you can't just hole up somewhere alone and never get close to anyone ever again. That's not living. That's not life."

Lane grabbed her shoulders. "I don't want to live! Don't you get that? I wish I was dead. Ever since they died, I wanted to die."

He sat down on the bed and cried into his hands. Wendy sat down beside him and put her arm around him. She rubbed his back and cried with him.

"I don't want to move on," Lane said, his head still in his hands. "Everyone wants me to heal and forget and get back to normal. But there is no normal for me anymore. And I don't want to forget about them. I don't want to be normal and not hurt. I'm scared if I stop hurting they'll just be a memory, they won't be real. They'll just be a picture in an album, almost fake. At least this way I know I had a wife, a baby. I don't want to forget them."

Wendy reached for one of his hands. "Lane, baby–"

He pushed her hand away. "That's why I have to leave. Because when I'm with you I feel good, I feel happy. I feel normal again. And I don't want that. I don't want that anymore. So I'll drink and I'll hurt you to make you go away. And I don't want to hurt you.

So leave. Get out so I can pack up and get out of here."

"Lane, please."

He raised his head and looked at her. His face was emotionless. Wendy got on her knees in front of him and grabbed his hands.

"Stay with me. We can do this together. We can help each other. I don't want you to forget. I just want you to live."

Lane looked away from her and pulled back his hands. "Just go, Wendy. Please."

Wendy stood up and left him there, sitting on the bed. She held back the tears and drove away slowly, hoping he would come after her. Forget wanting to be a happy couple and starting over and no longer being lonely. She was worried about Lane hurting himself and wondered if she should call the police. She stopped twice on the road and almost turned around. But she didn't, because she'd learned years ago that you couldn't help someone who didn't want it.

When she got home, she went straight to Granny and cried in the old woman's arms, like she'd done so many times before.

# Daryl

ark clouds were moving out of the west, which usually meant rain was on the way. It made Daryl's apartment look gray and depressing. But he didn't care about that, because Trisha was here. On his bed.

She'd come over for lunch, and after they ate, they went to the balcony and smoked a little. This time Daryl had cigarettes to offer. After a few minutes, though, Trisha complained about the heat and suggested they go to his bedroom. Daryl readily agreed.

Now they were sitting beside each other on the bed, Trisha occasionally stretching her long, tanned legs out. She leaned back on her hands and looked around at his room. Not that there was much to look at. He didn't have the money to decorate. But she seemed interested.

"I've never dated someone my own age," Trisha said. The comment was out of the blue, and Daryl didn't know how to respond. So he just looked interested and nodded.

"Older boys always liked me," she continued. "When I was in middle school the high school boys came around. When I was in high school the college boys came around. You know what I mean?"

Daryl didn't and his face must have said it.

"I'm just letting you know, this isn't weird for me," Trisha said. "Our age difference."

"Oh. Okay."

Trisha stretched her legs out again and looked over at him. Daryl wasn't sure what he should do. He hadn't dated in a long time and had never been with someone so young and so beautiful.

"We can kiss," Trisha said. "If you want."

Daryl nodded but didn't move. He felt paralyzed. Somehow he was able to lean toward her. She met him halfway, her scent sweeping over him just as her lips touched his. They were soft, and he was immediately concerned about many things. His lips being chapped, his breath being bad, not knowing how to kiss anymore.

But Trisha didn't say anything or stop. She kept kissing him. So he kissed her back. He put his hand on her bare thigh that was so tan and traced his fingers along the area where her shorts ended. She sighed softly and put her hand on the back of his neck.

Then she pulled away slightly. "Kiss my neck."

Daryl used his hand to gently lift up her chin and kissed her neck, from her collarbone up to her ear.

Trisha moaned. "More."

She was rubbing his scalp with her fingers, lightly pressing down her nails. Daryl took some of the soft skin of her neck into his lips and sucked in lightly. She moaned again. He nibbled a bit with his teeth and she seemed to like it, so he kept at it.

It went on like that for a while, until Daryl got overcome with the moment and grabbed one of her breasts. She quickly reached for his hand and pushed it away.

"I don't want to rush anything," she said. Daryl just nodded.

They kissed some more and then went to the balcony to smoke some more. The dark clouds had tempered the heat a little, but it was still humid. Daryl suggested they smoke inside but Trisha didn't want his apartment to smell like smoke.

After she finished one cigarette, Trisha left. Daryl stayed on the balcony and smoked another, watching the clouds drift closer and closer until the earth was shadowed. Maybe it would rain, but he had doubts. He couldn't trust the sky anymore.

# Melissa

"I know it can be hard, honey, but you just have faith," Sherry said. "God will get you through this."

"I know he will," Melissa answered. And she did know. From a young age she believed God existed and that miracles happened, and though she wasn't quite sure, she thought she might have a guardian angel. Things hadn't always been easy in her life, but she'd never been hungry or homeless or destitute. So she believed in God and had faith in him.

But she'd needed some encouragement, so she was here at Sherry's house, sitting in a perfectly clean kitchen. How did this woman clean her house so well? She didn't have a maid or any help like that. Something like that would make for extra juicy gossip, and Melissa would've heard long ago. She took another sip of perfect coffee from a perfect mug and put it back down on a perfect saucer. A saucer. Who used saucers for their coffee? The Rockefellers maybe.

"And you remember, you've got plenty of us to lean on here,"

Sherry said. "Don't be afraid to call any of the women at church. We'll be glad to listen, to be a shoulder to cry on. Okay?"

Melissa nodded. If she ever called any of those women it would set off a rumor mill big enough to shut down the phone lines for a few hours. She knew that for a fact. She'd gotten those calls before, someone telling her to pray for so-and-so because her husband cheated on her or left her or beat her. Now she was one of those so-and-so's.

"And I know this doesn't make sense right now, but God is gonna use this for his glory," Sherry said. "He is. Something is gonna come out of this, something that will make us shout 'hallelujah!' Just wait."

Melissa couldn't take anymore. "Sherry, I wish God could somehow get glory without destroying my life."

Sherry wrapped both of her hands around her coffee cup and held it up, like it was a shield. She looked shaken. Her eyes darted back and forth quickly.

"I didn't mean it like that," she said. "Of course he doesn't. He didn't. I mean, God didn't make Daryl leave or anything like that. I'm just saying, you've got to look on the bright side and trust that God will use this for his glory. For the kingdom. That's all."

"I just want my husband back. My little boy's father back. I just want my family back, Sherry. I don't care about God's glory. All I care about is getting my family back."

Melissa felt the tears flowing down her cheeks. She tried to say something more, but she couldn't get out the words. All that came out was a sob. Sherry got up and hugged her. It felt good at first, to have someone to hold her and tell her everything would be alright. But after a few seconds she started wondering if Sherry would use her as a teaching illustration one day in Sunday school.

When Sherry released her, Melissa stood up and grabbed her purse. "I should get going."

"No, honey, stay. I'm sorry. I didn't mean to upset you."

"It's okay, Sherry. Thanks for listening. I should go."

Melissa rushed out while Sherry tried to get her to stay. It felt rude but Sherry's house was starting to feel like a prison. A very clean prison. Melissa got in her car and drove home. The dark clouds hanging in the sky matched her mood and the thought occurred to her that she might never shake them.

She didn't want to wait around for God to make something good of the wreckage of her marriage. She didn't have time for that. Dustin didn't. He was almost thirteen, about to go through a time in his life when he needed a man around. And that man should be Daryl, even if she didn't consider him much of a man at the moment.

Melissa had never been afraid to make tough decisions. When her father was dying, in a coma for weeks and brain dead, and none of her siblings could even speak about pulling the plug, she brought it up. Talked it over with the doctor and signed the paperwork while they cried. She could live with consequences. She did what needed to be done. Always had.

Dustin needed his father and his mother, and Melissa would do what she had to so he would get that. Even if it meant throwing away her life, her happiness. Her baby would be happy. She could do that.

# Dustin

The clouds above looked dark. Like it was going to rain. There were even flashes of lightning. So Dustin decided to hustle home. It probably wouldn't rain, but the lightning was dangerous. And he was tired.

As he came out of the woods he saw Lane walking out of the trailer with a box. He took it to his truck and put it in the bed. Threw it in the bed, actually. Lane looked like he was in a hurry. Dustin ran as fast as he could until he reached Lane's truck. Lane came out of the trailer a minute later with a duffel bag on his shoulder and another box in his arms.

"What're you doing?" Dustin asked. Lane didn't answer. He just walked by and put the stuff in the truck.

"Lane!" Dustin shouted. "What're you doing?"

Lane turned and looked at him. "I'm leaving."

"What?"

"You heard me."

"Why?"

"I just have to," Lane said. "I can't explain. Don't have to. But I gotta go, bud."

Lane walked back into the trailer. Dustin followed him into the kitchen, where Lane had grabbed a trash bag. He was cleaning out the fridge, throwing old food and beer bottles into the trash bag.

"Why won't you tell me?" Dustin asked. "Are you mad at somebody? Are you mad at me?"

"It's not you, buddy. I can tell you that."

"Is it Wendy?"

Lane paused for a second, then shook his head. "No."

But Dustin thought he might be lying. "You can tell me why Lane. We're friends."

"You know, my mama would be pretty upset if she found out I had alcohol in this trailer," Lane said. "Make sure you don't say anything about it if they ever make it back around here."

"I thought we were friends," Dustin said.

"We are."

"Then tell me why you're leaving."

Lane stopped and looked back at him. "You're too young to understand, Dustin, and even if you weren't, I wouldn't trouble you with it. Don't want your heart to be heavy because of me."

"Is it my mom?"

Lane's eyes got wide. "What? No. Why do you ask that?"

"I heard her say your name when she was sleeping. She was dreaming. She was asking you for help."

Lane shook his head. "No, it's not your mom."

"Then why, Lane?"

Lane squatted down so that he was eye level with Dustin. "I came here for a reason, and it didn't work. I met some good people. You and your parents. Wendy. But that's not why I came here. I came to get away from people."

"You're running away from us," Dustin said.

"No."

"Yes, you are."

231

Lane sighed and turned back to fridge.

"You're scared," Dustin said. "You're scared so you're running away."

Lane didn't say anything, just kept cleaning out the fridge.

"I'm sorry you're leaving. Bye."

Dustin didn't wait for Lane to answer. He ran from the trailer, his backpack bouncing on his shoulders. As he ran up the road, the rain started to fall. A few tiny drops hit his forehead first, then fat drops started falling faster. Soon everywhere he looked was a blanket of water, falling so hard that he could barely see. The road beneath his feet turned to mud.

When he reached his house at the top of the hill, he saw his mom standing in the front yard. She was looking up at the sky and letting the rain fall on her. There was no way to tell for sure but it looked like she was crying. She looked beautiful.

She looked down and saw him watching her. She waved him over. Dustin ran to her, letting his backpack slide off of him. He practically jumped into her arms. She hugged him tighter than she ever had. She smelled like rain, and he loved it.

His mom let him go and looked down at him. "I love you, Dustin."

"I love you, too," he replied. He was glad it was raining so she couldn't see his tears.

She grabbed his hands and they danced in the front yard while heaven rained down around them. Dustin couldn't remember being happier.

# Lane

The rain poured down and washed out a lot of the roads. Lane shook his head as he sat in his truck watching the drops splatter on all over his windshield. Rain was rare this late in summer. This much rain was an absolute miracle. He was sitting outside of Wendy's house, trying to get up the courage to talk to her.

So far he wasn't doing too well.

He was sober. That was the problem. That little bender last night used all his liquor. Now he was just sitting in a truck outside someone's house like a crazy person. Wendy probably knew he was out there and was waiting for him to do something.

Nothing to lose, he decided. He got out of the truck and ran to the porch, but still got soaked. He knocked on the door and waited. It didn't take long for Wendy to answer.

She opened the door. "Hey."

"Can we talk?" Lane asked.

"You staying?"

"No."

"Then I don't have anything to say."

She tried to shut the door but Lane put his hand on it and stopped her. She poked her head from around the frame and glared at him.

"Stop it," Wendy said. "Don't cause trouble."

"I'm not. I just want to talk."

"And I want you to stay. But you're not. You don't always get what you want."

Lane felt like crying a little and shouting a little. Instead, he told her "I love you."

"What?" Wendy opened the door wider and looked at him, her mouth open a little.

"I love you," Lane said. "I do."

She didn't say anything. Just stared at him.

"Can I come in?" he asked. She nodded.

They went to the kitchen and sat down at the table. Usually Wendy was all manners, offering coffee or tea and a bite to eat. But not now. She just watched him like he was a snake that might bite her.

"It's why I've got to leave, Wendy." Lane reached out and took one of her hands. "It's like I told you back at the trailer. I'm gonna hurt you. That's why I'm out here by myself. I ran off my parents, my friends. Anyone who wanted to help me, to make me feel better. I don't want to feel better."

She tightened her grip on his hand. "Lane, I love you. I want you to be happy. I want you to live. I'm never gonna want anything different. Just stay here with me. Let's figure out a way for you to be happy. To live. Not forget your wife and baby. Never forget about them. But you're still living. God wants you to be alive. That's why you're still here. Here with me."

"If we end up happy, she'll be just a memory," Lane said. "That's it. And I can't have that. I can't let her go like that. I don't want to forget her."

Wendy stood up, still holding his hand. "Come with me."

234

Lane wanted to resist, tell her he was leaving and walk out. Leave Crow Valley and never come back. There was nothing for him here, no reason to come back. Except this woman. He followed her.

She led him to her bedroom and shut the door. "Sit on the bed."

Lane sat down on the bed. Wendy came and stood in front of him, put a hand on his cheek and stroked his skin. She took a step back and lifted her shirt over her head, then tossed the shirt on the bed. He looked at her, standing there in just her bra and some shorts. Her belly was flat and tiny ab muscles peek through her skin near her navel.

"Wendy, don't do this."

"Hush."

She reached behind her back and unhooked the bra, then turned around. On her back were thick, pink scars. They were all over, from her shoulders to the small of her back. She backed up to him so that he was close enough to touch. Lane reached out and ran his fingers over the raised skin. Over every single scar.

Wendy sat down beside him and hooked her bra back together. She put her head on his shoulder and sighed.

"My ex-husband's name was Nick," she said. "Not long after we got married, he started getting rough with me. Shoving me, slapping me every now and then. I knew it was wrong but I was young and very stupid. So I stayed with him."

Lane put his arm around her and pulled her close. She was crying while she talked. He wanted to pull her as close as he could, squeeze every ounce of pain out of her. For once, he was glad he was sober. He wanted to feel every moment with her.

"Then he started in with the drugs," she continued. "It got worse. So I finally told him I was leaving. He didn't take it well. Threw me down on the ground, dragged me by my hair to our garage. He cut off a piece of a heavy duty extension cord and beat me with it until I passed out."

Lane kissed her forehead. "I'm sorry."

"I woke up on the garage floor, bleeding. Hurting bad. I got

235

up, went inside. Found Nick asleep on the couch, so drugged out he was drooling. I watched him for a while, let him sleep. Then I decided I was gonna leave him."

Wendy looked up at him and actually smiled. "And this is the only funny part in this sad story. I went to the kitchen and got a cast iron skillet, then brought it down on his head. Just once. Banged him up pretty good. Anyway, I came after him with a frying pan. Just like in the movies. Or cartoons. Whatever. Nick's brain is a little bit slower now."

She took his hand. "My back healed up, but these scars are gonna be with me forever. I don't forget about them, even if they're healed. But I'm gonna keep living. I'm gonna love the people I love and hope that they'll love me back. That's all I want for you. You're never gonna forget them. Ever. Your scars are deeper than mine."

Wendy pushed herself back on the bed and laid back against some pillows. "Please stay with me."

She reached for his arm and when he felt her skin touch his, Lane realized he was crying. He crawled up into her arms and laid his head on her chest, his head moving up and down with every breath she took.

"I'll stay," he said.

# Wendy

Wendy woke up slowly, letting her consciousness drift in like the tide. She reached for Lane and didn't find him. She sat up and saw him by her bookshelf, looking through the titles. He looked better now, a day away from a drinking binge and with a good night's sleep. One day she and him would sleep together every night.

"Morning," he said.

"Good morning."

"You have a lot of books," he said. "Most of them I've never heard of."

"I like them."

Lane grabbed a couple and sat down on the side of the bed. "Like these. I can't even pronounce the name of these. *Oedipus Rex. The Oresteia. Antigone.*"

"They're Greek plays. Classics."

"They may be classics but I still can't pronounce them."

He set the books down on the ground and kissed her. His whiskers scratched her face but she liked it. She made sure to keep her mouth closed because she hadn't brushed her teeth.

"Why do you like them?" Lane asked.

Wendy thought for a moment. "It's like they break down life into something you can understand. They're tragedies. Good things happen, then bad things happen. Like in real life. It's kind of a way to understand human nature."

"Alright."

"Maybe I'm just a nerd."

"Maybe." Lane inched closer to her. "I think you just like depressing stories."

"No, it's not that. There's hope in them. That's what I like."

Lane put his arm around her. "I don't think I'll be reading them anytime soon."

"Some of them are lame, I'll admit," Wendy said. "A lot of them do this thing where the main character will get painted into a corner. No way out, right? And then something miraculous will happen. Like a god will descend out of the sky and save them. Just like that, for no reason, other than the writer was a hack and couldn't come up with a good way to end it."

"Huh."

"It's called deus ex machina."

"What?"

"It's Latin," Wendy said. "It means 'god out of the machine.' Those Greek playwrights would have an actor playing a god descend onto the stage using a machine. So that's where you get the phrase. Like I said, it's kind of a lame way to end a good story."

"I'll take your word for it. I'll stick to the Grisham novels."

Wendy laughed. "So Granny has probably already seen your truck and figured out you spent the night here."

"Am I in trouble?"

"Depends on if she's having a good day or bad day."

"Okay."

They slowly walked to the kitchen together. Granny was

sitting at the kitchen table, sipping out of a coffee mug. She smiled at them and they sat down. Wendy felt embarrassed.

"Good morning," Granny said.

"Morning," Lane replied. Wendy said nothing. Granny just looked back and forth between both of them.

"My mind ain't what it used to be," she said. "But I am aware of what goes on in my own house."

"Nothing happened, Granny," Wendy said. "I promise."

"Honey, you're a grown woman. You can do what you want. Just don't come walking in here like the cat who ate the canary."

Granny smiled at them. Wendy smiled back, wanting to hug her grandmother so tight. She looked at Lane who still looked embarrassed.

"Now, I'm hungry," Granny said. "And I don't believe I've had the pleasure of eating anything Lane has cooked."

"I don't know if you would call it a pleasure," Lane said. "But I'll see what I can whip up."

Lane made breakfast for the three of them. They sat and talked for more than an hour. Wendy couldn't help but picture a family, and she loved that Lane wanted to be a part of it.

# Daryl

More than two weeks had gone by since Trisha had come to his apartment. Daryl missed touching her skin and her thin, soft lips. But mostly he missed the companionship. The silence of his apartment was killing him. He'd broke down and cried the last two nights. This was what he wanted, though. Some space.

Last weekend had been good. Dustin had come over Saturday morning and they spent the day together. They saw a movie, went fishing, and got ice cream. It was one of the better days they'd had together in a long time. And it felt good to have someone in the apartment with him. Dustin slept on the floor in a sleeping bag, and it felt like when Daryl was a young kid and had friends over.

But through it all, Daryl's mind remained on Trisha. Why hadn't she returned a call? Why was she avoiding him? Maybe she hadn't enjoyed their make out session like he had. It was possible he was a bad kisser. He'd only kissed Melissa for the last twenty years.

Maybe she didn't realize how bad he was at kissing, at sex. Maybe she didn't care and loved him anyway.

He went to Shelley's first looking for Trisha. She wasn't there. Luckily the other waitresses knew him, recognized him as Trisha's friend. They gave him directions to her house and said she might be there. Said she'd been talking about him a lot while she was at work. Daryl took that as a good sign.

He drove over to Trisha's house and parked out front. It was a modest little house with white clapboard siding that needed some paint. The grass needed mowing, too. There was a red Pontiac out front. Not Trisha's. Unless she'd bought a new car in the last couple of weeks. Daryl got out of his truck and started walking up to the door.

Before he could get there, though, a man in his late twenties came out of the door. He was ragged-looking, with a scraggly beard and bloodshot eyes. His hair looked like it hadn't been combed in a while, and he was wearing a white t-shirt with stains on the chest.

"Just stop right there," the man said. Daryl stopped as the man walked over to him.

"I'm looking for Trisha," Daryl said.

"I figured." The man spit near Daryl's shoes. "So you're the guy she's been messing around with?"

"What?"

"Yeah, I thought so," the man said. "You don't even know. Look here, man. I'm her boyfriend. Curtis. Maybe she said something about me?"

Daryl didn't respond, so Curtis shrugged his shoulders and continued. "She was just using you, man. To make me jealous. To get me to propose. Anyway, we're getting married now. Probably why she stopped answering your calls."

Daryl just stared at Curtis. He didn't know what to say. This man was talking with him about this like it was current events or the score of a baseball game. Just something that happened.

"Never slept with you, did she?" Curtis asked, then spit again. "Yeah, she's a tease. She acts like she's loose but nope. Gotta buy her

241

stuff, man. Anyway, when she came home with that hickey on neck, I knew she was serious. She forced my hand, man. Or I guess you did. So I went to Wal-Mart and bought her a ring. That's why she's not answering your calls, man. And why you're here. Right?"

Daryl nodded.

"Yeah, man, she was just messing with me. I guess I don't have a problem with you, but don't come around here no more. Alright? She don't want you. And I ain't scared to get rough with you, man. You come around again, and we'll get to it. Understand?"

Daryl just nodded and stumbled back to his truck. He wasn't really scared of the little punk. Daryl was actually bigger than him. But the boy looked like he wanted to fight just for the sake of fighting. And Daryl didn't want to get into it. It wouldn't look right for a game warden to get into a fist fight over a woman. A woman that wasn't his wife. Trisha wasn't worth it.

He drove back to his apartment fast, going way over the speed limit. She used him. He kept thinking it. She used him to get Curtis to propose to her. Fine. Daryl wasn't heartbroken. It wasn't like he was in love with Trisha, this young girl with whom he had nothing in common. No it wasn't that. He just felt foolish.

Daryl went to his bedroom in his dark, quiet apartment and laid down on the bed. He turned the radio up as loud as he could and cried. For the third night in a row he broke down and sobbed. Cried like a baby. Cried like his daddy told him a man never should. Cried out to God and begged for forgiveness for so many things that it just ended up being the babbling of a pathetic child.

242

# Melissa

elissa had turned around three times on the way. Just coming here made her angry and hurt all over again, and she didn't want to do it. But she'd made a decision and was going to do it. Dustin needed a father, and she was willing to do anything to make sure her son had a family. Even if it meant swallowing her pride and anger.

She knocked on the door and waited for Daryl to answer. She knew he was here. His truck was in the parking lot. When they got married all those years ago, Melissa never thought she would be outside her husband's apartment, waiting to talk to him. Never imagined having the family they worked to build broken in two. Never.

After a few moments she heard the deadbolt slide and Daryl opened the door. He looked terrible. His face was pale and dark circles were under his eyes. Melissa wondered when he last showered. He looked surprised to see her, and she didn't blame him.

"Melissa."

"Can we talk?" she asked.

Daryl nodded and stepped back, letting her in. She looked around and felt sad for him. It was empty and made her feel empty and she was sure Daryl felt the same. He motioned her over to a card table, one she recognized from their storage shed. They sat down across from each other on two cheap chairs. She didn't want to know where he got them.

"Where's Dustin?" he asked.

"He's at the house with Lane and Wendy. I asked them to watch him. Seemed like they were itching to play house."

Daryl nodded. "Is he alright? Is that why you're here?"

"No, he's fine. Nothing's wrong."

Daryl sighed and looked relieved. Melissa watched him for a couple of seconds, looked at the lines in his face. He looked old. Well, not old. But he looked like a man in his forties, and she thought that she probably looked like a woman in her forties. For some reason, she'd had this picture of the two of them in her mind, and that picture was of two young kids, facing life together. They weren't kids anymore.

"Are you okay?" Daryl asked.

Melissa thought for a moment. "No."

He didn't respond. She could tell he wasn't surprised.

"Why'd you come by?" he asked.

Melissa took a deep breath. "I want you to come home."

He nodded like he understood but didn't say anything. Just sat there.

"Buy your boat," she said. "We'll give you some space. I forgive you. For leaving, for the other woman. For all of it. And I'm sorry for what I did wrong. I'm sorry for ignoring what you needed. I'm sorry for not taking care of our relationship. I am. But I want you to come home."

"Okay."

Melissa looked at him with surprise. She'd thought it would take convincing. She had been prepared to beg. To argue and cajole.

244

But here he was, agreeing just like that.

"What?" he asked.

"I just...I thought you liked it here."

Daryl stood up and ran a hand through his thinning hair. Rubbed his neck with the same hand. He looked so tired. Did he look that tired when he lived at home?

"This was a mistake," he said. "The whole thing. I was...I don't know. Stir crazy? Felt trapped. Not really by you or Dustin. Just by life. Doing the same thing, day after day. That's all."

"Oh." Melissa didn't say anything else. Just waited for him to go on.

"I'm sorry, too," he said. "I shouldn't have left. I should've stayed. I'm sorry."

He started crying and sat down at the table with her. She just let him cry, didn't try to comfort him. Just let it happen.

"I forgive you," she said. "But I'm still mad. I'm still so angry with you."

"I know." He sobbed some more. "I know."

"I'm willing to try, though."

"Okay."

After that she reached for his hand. He took hers and he squeezed it tight, so tight it hurt. She waited for him to calm down before she spoke.

"This is for Dustin," Melissa said. "You understand that, right?"

Daryl nodded.

"Okay."

"So what do we do?" he asked.

Melissa thought for a moment. "Let's start with supper tonight. You come home for supper. We'll go from there."

"Okay."

She told him to shower and waited for him on the balcony. It smelled like smoke, and she realized Daryl had been out here smoking. She shook her head and rolled her eyes. When he was out of the shower and cleaned up and looking better, they left the apartment in separate vehicles, headed home.

The whole drive Melissa wondered if she was doing the right thing. She wouldn't be happy, wouldn't be living that fairytale life every little girl dreams about. But her son would have his father. That mattered. She kept telling herself that, even said it out loud. But she still felt empty inside.

Yes, her husband was coming home, but she didn't feel happy about it. Melissa cried the whole way home.

# Dustin

The morning had been pretty good, but Dustin was getting restless. His mom left early with a look on her face that told him she was going to see his dad. It was the same look she had when his grandma died a few years ago. Her serious face is what Dustin called it.

He'd told his mom he didn't need any adults around to watch him. Begged her. He was almost thirteen. He wasn't helpless. But she'd insisted. It worked out, though, because Lane and Wendy were here with him. They all went to town and got some snacks that Dustin wanted, like chicken nuggets and ice cream. Then they came home and played some board games. It was fun, even if Lane and Wendy were kind of flirting with each other a lot.

But now he wanted to get out of the house. He loved the woods, always had. Maybe because his dad was a game warden. When Dustin grew up, he wanted to be a park ranger at a national park. Maybe Yosemite. Or Yellowstone. And he wanted to find the panther. School started in a few weeks.

After lunch, he asked them if he could go to the woods. To his surprise, Lane and Wendy asked if they could go with him. He quickly agreed and got together his stuff. But Wendy wanted to pack snacks for them, and of course Lane thought it was a good idea. Dustin asked if he could go ahead of them and meet them at the creek near an old beaver's dam. There was usually a great blue heron there around noon, hunting fish where the water pooled up. He wanted to see it.

They told him to go ahead and they would catch up. Dustin smiled big and ran out the door. With three pairs of eyes, maybe they'd see the panther today. Even though Wendy was a girl, she might be good at finding animals. He ran the dirt road as fast as he could, dust flying up behind his sneakers.

# Lane

Lane kissed Wendy on the cheek and followed Dustin outside. Having some food sounded like a good idea to him, but going through someone else's pantry and fridge made him feel weird.

So he let Wendy rummage through the kitchen and find the snacks. He walked out to the road and stood there watching Dustin run down the hill. It made him laugh. Lane remembered being that excited, that happy about life.

He turned to go back inside, wishing he had a cigarette, when out of the corner of his eye he saw some movement down the hill. He looked back just in time to see Dustin disappearing into the trees beside the road, being pulled by a skinny older man Lane didn't recognize. His heart instantly drummed in his chest and he got dizzy.

"Wendy!" he screamed as loud as he could. "Wendy!"

Wendy came running out the front door, a box of granola bars in her hand. She looked terrified, so the tone of his voice worked.

"Call 911!" Lane screamed to her. "Someone took Dustin! I saw a man take Dustin! Call the police!"

She looked at him for a second, like she didn't understand or believe him. Then she nodded and dropped the box of granola bars before going back inside. Lane started running down the hill as fast as he could. He heard Wendy yelling behind him to stop. But he couldn't.

# Victor

The little boy was skinny but strong. Victor had to hold him tight. The boy wasn't scared, either. He fought back, clawing and scratching at Victor's arms. It was no use, though. Not only was Victor strong, he had a mission. A purpose. He no longer had to wait.

He didn't say anything to the boy. No need. No threats or promises. The boy was going to die, no matter what. He had seen what Victor needed to hide, or at least gotten too close, and would soon lead others there. The Great Underneath had given the boy to Victor. There was no escaping death now.

Victor took the boy to the place where he'd dumped the old man. He leaned the boy up against a large oak tree near the water hole and duct taped his feet together. Victor didn't like binding up his victims. But he couldn't chance the boy running away. Victor had some things to do before he took the boy's life.

"Do you know where you are?" Victor asked.

The boy said nothing, but looked him in the eye. Steady gaze. Victor was impressed.

"You know. You've seen it before. You've seen the old man, right?"

The boy shook his head, look confused. It didn't matter. His soul belonged to Victor now. Belonged to the Underneath. Victor walked over to another tree and grabbed a cooler he'd placed there hours before. He walked back over to the boy and set the cooler down in front of him.

Victor took out the large hunting knife and the giant rat. Now the boy's eyes got big and a shiver passed through him. Now the boy understood what was happening. Soon he would know what it all meant.

# Wendy

Wendy cried into the phone, trying to explain to the 911 operator what had happened and where she was. She didn't know the address. There weren't any addresses this far outside of town. Just county road numbers and private road numbers. She looked through the house to find some of Daryl and Melissa's mail. When she finally located some, it had a PO box address. They got their mail in town.

Dustin had been taken. That was all she knew. And Lane had gone after him. Lane was alone in the woods, with no weapon or anything, against a man who took a little boy against his will. The man probably had a weapon. God, he probably had a gun.

Wendy stayed on the line while the operator talked to her, trying to calm her down. The police would be there, the operator was telling her. Soon. Just give them time. Wendy collapsed into the couch and sobbed. The operator said some things and Wendy ignored them. Dustin and Lane were alone in the woods with someone dangerous. That was all she could think of.

Then the door opened. She looked up and saw Daryl and Melissa. She started crying all over again and ran to Melissa.

"I'm sorry, I'm sorry," Wendy said between sobs. It was all she could get out. Daryl asked what was wrong. He put his hand on her shoulder and it steadied her a bit.

Melissa looked horrified. Wendy understood then that mothers knew when something happened to their children. She tried to explain between her gasps for air.

# Daryl

Something was wrong. Daryl knew it when he pulled into the drive. He wondered what it was that made people be able to tell when something bad had happened. Did tragedy leave something in the air? When he came inside and saw Wendy crying on the couch, he knew it was bad.

The girl ran over to them, sobbing, trying to tell them what happened. He put his hand on her shoulder to calm her down.

"What's wrong?" he asked her.

"Someone took Dustin," she answered. She wiped her eyes. "He was walking down the road and a man took him. Into the woods."

Melissa staggered backwards. Daryl grabbed her shoulders and steadied her, then helped her onto the couch. Wendy sat down with her. He noticed the phone in Wendy's hand.

"You called the police?" he asked.

Wendy nodded.

"Where's Lane?"

"He went after them," she replied.

Daryl squatted so that he was on eye level with Wendy and Melissa. "Tell the police I'll leave a trail. Tell them to follow the trail. I'll make it obvious. Okay?"

They both nodded. Daryl went to the bedroom and looked in the night stand beside the bed for the gun he kept there. He'd left it for Melissa, in case anything happened. But it was gone. He went back to the living room.

"Where's the gun?" he asked Melissa.

"In the night stand drawer."

He shook his head. "It's gone."

Melissa closed her eyes. "Dustin."

"I'm going."

Daryl ran out the door and down the road. On the left side of the road was a field. On the right was a deep forest that stretched behind their property and Lane's. It was where Dustin ran around all the time. It was where he'd been taken. Daryl searched the trees on the side of the road for any sign and, after a few minutes, found it. A small pine sapling that was snapped in two, freshly broken.

He climbed the embankment and went into the woods. He was grateful for the little bit of tracking experience he had. Thank God he loved hunting. And thank God for Dustin. The little boy was struggling, thrashing around. Daryl found broken twigs and branches every few yards. And footprints every now and then. Only one set. Dustin was being carried.

Daryl followed the trail deeper into the woods, snapping tree branches and leaving large marks in any mud he found.

# Melissa

Her baby. That's all Melissa could think about. The one she spent sixteen hours in labor to deliver. The one she fed and rocked to sleep at night. The little boy with scrapes on his knees and elbows, who smelled of sweat and earth and pine. She remembered every hug, every kiss. Now he was gone, and she didn't know how to help him.

Wendy moved closer and wrapped her in a hug. They cried together as Melissa waited to hear sirens. She prayed that God would keep her family safe.

# Dustin

The man who took him had his back turned to Dustin, performing some sort of ritual. He was cleaning his hands using soap and a gallon jug of water. He just kept washing his hands over and over. And chanting.

Dustin didn't know why the man wanted to kill him, but he knew he was serious. The man's eyes were glazed over and dilated. Maybe he was on drugs. Whatever the reason, he wasn't joking and hadn't said anything about ransom or returning Dustin. He'd barely said anything at all.

He let his backpack slide off his shoulders slowly so that it didn't make any noise hitting the ground. With his hands behind him, he reached into the backpack and found the gun. He pulled it out and felt for the safety and clicked it off. The man was still washing his hands and face, so Dustin brought the gun around his body until it laid on the ground beside his leg. He pushed it toward a mix of grass and leaves so it was hidden.

The man had to get closer. Dustin wasn't sure he could hit him from this far away. And he couldn't miss. He would have to wait until the man was right upon him to fire. So Dustin waited while the man washed and chanted.

# Lane

L ane had no experience tracking. He'd been hunting before, for deer and hogs, but that was it. Right now he was relying on some broken tree limbs and a few footprints in the dirt.

Mostly he prayed he would find Dustin before it was too late.

He moved as fast as he could, tripping over fallen logs and holes in the ground. Spider webs hit him the face. He stayed along the creek that ran the length of the woods, hoping to hear something. A cough, a sneeze, Dustin's voice. Something to tell him he was going in the right direction.

And then he saw them. Lane came out of a group of trees into a small clearing. He recognized it instantly. It was where he sprained his ankle hunting with Dustin. The man and Dustin were down by the creek, where the trees started growing thick again. Dustin was sitting up against a tree, and the man was washing his hands.

Lane picked up his speed and ran straight toward the man.

He had no plan and no weapon. He didn't know if the man had a weapon. But he couldn't wait. There was no telling how long it would take the police to get out this far. If Dustin was going to live, Lane was going to have to save him.

The man finally saw him when Lane was a few yards away, but it was too late by then. Lane took a few more strides and then barreled into the man, trying to remember the proper tackling form he learned playing football in high school. He wrapped his arms around the man, putting his full weight into him.

But the man was strong and agile for his age. And he knew what he was doing. He took Lane's weight and rolled, throwing him to the side. The momentum carried Lane a few feet away from the man and stunned him for a second. That was all the man needed. He was on Lane in an instant and punched him in the throat, then in his torso right below the sternum.

Lane gasped for air, grabbing his throat. It felt like all the air had left his lungs and nothing else was coming back in. He rolled onto his side, trying to take deep breaths. Trying to get up.

The man calmly walked over to a cooler near Dustin and pulled out a large hunting knife. Its blade gleamed in the afternoon sun. He smiled and started walking over Lane.

# Daryl

aryl came out of the woods to a clearing and saw them all. He was too late. He hadn't got there soon enough.

A man he didn't recognize was standing over Lane, a bloody hunting knife in his hand. And Dustin was sitting against a tree, holding a gun. The gun that was supposed to be in the night stand by Daryl's bed.

"I'll shoot you!" Dustin yelled. "Get away from him!"

The man turned and looked at Dustin. A strange smile spread across his face as he looked down at the boy. Daryl started walking forward slowly. No one had noticed him yet. He hoped he would be able to attack the man from behind. But he was still too far away, about twenty yards.

"Drop the knife and go away!" Dustin yelled again. "I'll shoot you!"

The man took a step toward Dustin. "Do you think you can, little boy? Can you take a life that hasn't been given to you?"

"Stop it!"

Daryl held his breath and stepped slowly, getting closer and closer. Lane saw him now, but stayed focused on the man. He was holding his throat and breathing heavily. Daryl couldn't tell if he was alright.

"Your life has already been given to me, boy," the man said. "You won't shoot. You can't take what hasn't been given to you."

The man took another step and Daryl clenched his fists. The man was still too close to Dustin. Daryl wouldn't be able to reach him before the man could get to Dustin. But Daryl had to do something. It looked like Lane was injured, but maybe if Daryl could get the man down, Lane could help. At least Dustin might be able to get away.

"You'll die, boy," the man said. "Just like the others."

Daryl started to run toward them as the man raised his knife and lunged toward Dustin, screaming something Daryl didn't understand. The gun went off in Dustin's hands, fire and smoke belching from the barrel. A black form descended from the tree Dustin leaned against, so fast it was a blur.

The panther Dustin had been hunting.

It leapt onto the man and tore at his throat. The man dropped his knife, the only defense he had, and grabbed the panther's head, trying to pull it away. Blood started pouring down everywhere. The man collapsed as the panther bit again and again.

"Why are you doing this, my god?" he screamed.

The man stopped clutching the panther's head, and his arms fell by his side. The panther grabbed one limp arm and dragged the man into the woods.

# Melissa

Melissa was standing on the porch with Wendy, waiting for the police, when she heard the gun shot ring out through the air. It echoed through the woods behind her house, finding its way through the air to her.

She fell to her knees and screamed so loud she could barely hear the sirens approaching.

# Dustin

is dad held him in his lap, like when he was a little kid. Dustin could tell his dad wanted to cry but was holding it in. Dustin wanted to cry, too. But there were policemen all around and he wanted to look tough.

Mostly, though, he was glad his dad had seen the panther. Lane, too. They believed him now. Well, Lane always believed him. But it felt better to have two other witnesses. Two people who could say they saw the panther. Two grownups that everyone would believe.

"You sure you're okay?" his dad asked. It was the tenth time he'd asked it.

"Yes," Dustin replied. "I promise."

His dad ran his fingers through Dustin's hair and hugged him again. The police wanted to ask Dustin some questions, but his dad told them to wait. Dustin was glad. He didn't have any answers for them. He didn't know why the man had taken him or why he planned to kill him. He'd never seen the man before in his life. At least not that he could remember.

They hadn't found the man's body yet. Dustin didn't think they would.

One of the older policemen wandered over, and his dad called out to him. "When's the ambulance coming?"

"About five minutes out," the old policeman answered.

"Who's that?" Dustin's dad nodded toward a tall man in a suit jacket and a cowboy hat. He stood still, calmly watching all the policemen move around busily.

"Texas Ranger," the old policeman replied. "New to the area. He was in the office when we got the call. Said he wanted to tag along."

Dustin's dad nodded. The old policeman wandered off. Dustin looked around for Lane and found him leaning up against the oak tree. He smiled at Dustin and waved. Dustin waved back.

"Lane's okay, right?" he asked his dad.

"He's fine. Just a few bruises."

"Okay."

His dad pressed Dustin's head into his chest and hugged him tight again. "I love you, Dustin. I love you."

"I love you, too, Dad." Dustin lifted his head off of his dad's chest. "Dad?"

"What?"

"Can you take me home?"

His dad nodded and picked Dustin up, setting him on his feet. He took Dustin's hand and led him over to the old policeman. They spoke quickly and the old policeman nodded. Then Dustin and his dad walked home through the woods to their home on the hill.

# Lane

Wendy fussed over him for a while, and Lane had to admit he liked it. She took him back to her house and made him lay on the couch. She let him pick out some movies and they watched them together. Granny made a big supper, and they all ate around the TV while watching *The Last Picture Show*.

Later, they went to Wendy's room and she read to him. Lane couldn't remember when he liked books so much. He closed his eyes and listened to Wendy's voice, and he fell asleep because it was like a song, the kind your mother sings to you when you're a baby.

Lane didn't dream at all while he slept. No demons, no screams or terror. Just sleep, pure rest and comfort while Wendy spoke over him.

# Wendy

After a while, Wendy noticed Lane was asleep. She set down the book she was reading and crawled into bed with him. It was hard to forget about the day, forget about how she almost lost him. But she did, because he was here now and he wasn't leaving. She knew that.

With her head on his chest, rising and falling with every breath he took, she thought about the future for the first time. Not something she imagined. A real future with Lane as her husband and at least one baby and maybe two. They would grow old together, and he would be kind to her, and she would be kind back.

Wendy traced Lane's hand with her fingers. This was the man she had pictured when she was a young girl. Not perfect, but the man she waited for. He was broken and so was she. They would put each other back together, piece by piece.

She closed her eyes, and they slept together until the sun rose on a new day.

# Daryl

Just a few boxes remained unpacked. Daryl sat down on the bed and rested for a minute. His bed. The bed he shared with his wife. Melissa was at the grocery store with Dustin, picking up some food for supper. They'd helped a little with the unpacking, both of them smiling. Daryl turned in the keys to the apartment the day before, paying the fee to break his lease early.

He walked into Dustin's room. It was a little messy, like a boy's room should be. A large branch leaned up against the wall in the corner. Daryl didn't know where it came from or why Dustin brought it home. The encyclopedias were still on the floor, along with some baseball cards and a glove.

Daryl went to the kitchen, poured a glass of sweet tea, and then went to the porch. He sat down and listened to the birds singing. He waited for the sound of Melissa's car, the sound of his family coming home. A family he'd almost lost. He closed his eyes and thanked God for them.

# Melissa

Melissa rolled over and put her arm around Daryl. She said a prayer to a God she wasn't even sure existed a month ago. A prayer of thanks. She still wasn't convinced he answered prayers. At least not all of them. There was too much hurt, too much pain in the world to be sure of that. But she knew that her family was together, even if it wasn't whole. She was thankful for that, at least.

Daryl snored slightly, and Melissa rubbed his back until he stopped. She was still angry with him, with how foolish and immature he'd been. He claimed he only kissed that girl and part of Melissa believed him. But a man in his situation would probably say anything to come back home. And it was Melissa who put the offer on the table with no conditions. She didn't ask for the complete truth or Daryl's whole heart. She only asked him to come home, and he did.

Melissa pulled him tight to her body and fell asleep. The sun broke through the windows in the morning and woke her to the first day with her family put back together. Now that she knew how easily it could fall apart, she felt grateful to have it again. She felt scared, a little unsure about life now. Everything felt simple before, but after this summer, it all seemed so fragile.

Doubt had crept into her mind, but Melissa did her best to ignore it. This morning was new, and she would be grateful for every moment of it.

# Lane

Night was coming. The days were growing shorter, the wind bringing the chill of autumn. Lane and Dustin sat on the porch of Lane's trailer, watching Wendy throw a ball to Dustin's new dog, a tan ridgeback with wide eyes. She played with the dog more than Dustin did, and Lane knew it wouldn't be long until she bought one of her own.

Lane leaned back in the chair and sighed, feeling at peace for the first time in years. He needed to get a job and start working. Maybe he'd open a repair shop, work on cars. He liked that. He still had enough money from selling his shop in Houston, but pretty soon he'd be buying a ring for Wendy. He couldn't live off his savings forever.

He stared off into the woods and said a prayer that everything would be alright. As he listened to a mockingbird's call, something moving caught his eye. At the edge of the woods, standing still and watching them, was the panther. Only its tail moved, switching back and forth.

Lane nudged Dustin and nodded toward the panther. It took him a few seconds, but then Dustin saw it. He smiled and shook his head. It watched them for more than hour, even laid down and seemed to doze. They kept an eye on it, but Lane never worried about it. He couldn't say why, but he didn't feel the need.

For years afterward, that panther would appear at the edge of the woods and sit with them, its yellow eyes watching every move they made. It saw Dustin grow into a man, Lane and Wendy's two children grow into teenagers. And then it one day it was gone, lost to those woods forever.

**Ben Zajdel** is the author of one previous novel and is a graduate of the University of Texas at Dallas. You can keep up with him at www.benzajdel.com. He lives in Dallas, Texas.

# Also by Ben Zajdel

## Fiction

Leaving Darkness

## Poetry

What Heaven Heard

# Leaving Darkness

Joshua Franklin is returning to Crow Valley, the place he grew up. Haunted by dreams of his high school sweetheart, Kathryn, he hopes this trip down memory lane will give him peace. Instead, he finds a nightmare. Separated for years, Josh and his friends are drawn together by the tragic death of their friend, Jason. Soon they are all finding menacing letters and dodging bullets, making them wonder if Jason's death was really an accident. When a former teacher with a grudge shows up at the funeral, they all begin to understand that the secrets they buried long ago have been unearthed, threatening to destroy their lives.

The only thing keeping Josh in town is a beautiful waitress who seems to have secrets of her own. But complicating things is his tumultuous relationship with Kathryn, who seems to simultaneously love and hate him. Leaving Darkness is the story of one man stepping out of his broken past and into the light of forgiveness.

# What Heaven Heard

This collection of poetry from Ben Zajdel covers a variety of subjects. Love, baseball, war, and tragedy are just a few of the topics found in these pages. These poems invite the reader to reflect on some of life's most significant events while also pausing to appreciate the ordinary ones. Find out how an old woman holding a flower can lead to tears of conviction. Discover if true love is really worth the wreckage it leaves in its wake. Imbued with heart and the imagery of East Texas, these poems capture what it means to live and love in an era of change.